METAL ANGELS

PART TWO

BY

D K GIRL

Metal Angels by Danielle K Girl

Cover Design: Jake Clark
Editor: Inspired Ink Editing
ISBN-13: 978-0-9981427-9-1

For Mikie.

This is really happening. I wish you were here to see it.

Blake - 21

The thin silver needle guided thread in and out of Blake's torn skin. Blood stained the tips of the nurse's gloved fingers as he sutured the wound on her palm.

'Are you all right?' The man, Jeremy according to his high-security pass, did not lift his gaze from his work.

'I'm fine.' Dirty and exhausted. Body shaking as though she were still in the middle of the tremendous earth tremor that had wracked the level eleven chamber just on an hour ago. When the gallu had arrived during the Final Meld, her body had ignited, the toxins in her blood becoming a raging heat beneath her skin. But now, with the Waters settled once again, the hollow ache at her core began to spread, clawing up out of her diaphragm and reaching for her ribs. Distant whispers played in her ears. Jeremy could not help her with those injuries. 'Are they taking Tamas somewhere?'

She nodded past the two armed guards – her escort Captain Nex's mandatory condition if she were to be allowed from his sight – who waited outside her compartment. In another compartment on the far side of the level three medical ward, Cym leaned over an unconscious Tamas. Another nurse and a doctor were with him. Their nodding heads indicated they had all come to an agreement of some kind.

'The director is going to be prepped for surgery up in the Zahra Centre,' Jeremy said. 'They need to reset his wrist.'

The Zahra Centre was a state-of-the-art on-site medical centre, built at the end of Tamas's mother's cancer battle and given her name. A staff perk that also removed the necessity for Tamas to leave the Facility when he was ill. Blake struggled to recall when she or Tamas had last left the high fences of their desert-bound workplace.

'And the head wound?' she said.

'Sutured, should be fine. He's been sedated for now, till surgery is done.' Jeremy paused, needle hovering above the last section of torn skin at the base of her thumb. 'That was quite a bang down there.'

Blake may not, according to Kira, have any social skills whatsoever, but that did not mean she was oblivious to a tremor in a voice, sweat beading on an upper lip. Jeremy wanted some reassurance that the Facility wasn't going to collapse on itself. That they weren't going to be buried alive or snuffed out by toxic smoke rising through the ventilation system.

'You're not going to die, if that is what's concerning you,' she said. Her gaze drifted to Perry in the compartment alongside hers. He lay still, surrounded by an array of machines that kept him alive. Beyond him lay Gren. The Syranian's compartment held only one piece of equipment: a narrow tube of translucent piping that haloed the crown of his head. A rainbow of colours filtered through the tube. Gren's injuries were covered by a foil blanket tucked up high around his neck. His body, no doubt, had already begun to heal at an accelerated rate.

'No, Miss Beckworth,' Jeremy sat back, needle and thread dangling, 'That's not what . . .'

'Of course it's what you wanted to know. Can you please finish up? I have things to do.'

Speaking so harshly to someone with a needle poised over your skin was perhaps not wise, but Blake was too distracted to curb her tongue. The damage to the carapaces was to her advantage. The list of repairs they required would ensure she was not thrown into a holding cell anytime soon, despite the captain's reassurances that would happen if she so much as blinked oddly.

Bottom line was, he needed her. The Meld had played havoc with the inhibitor system, torn ceramic eyes from sockets, ripped faux skin from limbs, and made the gallu far from ready for their public *close-up*. Cosmetic enhancement was required. And she was the senior make-up artist.

Jeremy returned to the job at hand. Though Blake's hand had been numbed, the last few digs of the needle seemed to penetrate deeper than before. She looked away, gritting her teeth against the odd sensation.

Just as the captain was gambling on allowing her some freedom, Blake was taking chances too. She could have fled in the chaos, but she remained and assisted with bringing the inhibitors back online. Keeping herself visible, so that Rossiter would have a chance to get out. And find Kira.

The serum Captain Nex had ordered Cym to inject her with had been far more powerful than anything human made. It had ripped truths from her—some terrible and personal— but the invasion only went so deep. She had ordered Kira to go to Melgrove, that much was true. Blake had ordered her sister to a place that held memories rich with pain, and hedged everything on the notion that Kira would not take one step in the place. That was the one truth the captain had not stolen from her.

'And we're done.' Jeremy wasted no time scooping up his equipment and striding from the compartment. He advised her guards that she was ready, and the two women turned in near-perfect unison.

'Wait,' Blake said. 'I want to speak with Cym before we go back down. I have some questions for him about the repairs.'

The larger of the two women, one Blake recalled passing once or twice in hallways, took little convincing and directed her angst-faced colleague to return to door-guarding duty. Whether they believed the official company line that the Syranians were genetically enhanced soldiers, or whether they leaned towards the rumour of extraterrestrial origins, one thing certain was that these guards would follow Captain Nex's directives in Tamas's absence. Blake's brain and technological prowess may ensure that their paychecks were covered by incoming contracts, but her position of power faded to nothing in the face of Nex's authoritative air. Blake was certain Captain Nex was capable of intimidating even the gods he and Tamas spent so much time praying to, if he so wished.

Blake rose to her feet, flexing her fingers. The black tiles beneath her seemed to rise and dip like onyx waves. She clutched the edge of the bed.

'Blake? Is everything all right?'

The question was getting tedious, and considering Cym was doing the asking, it was a ridiculous one at that.

'No, Cym. I'm fairly certain nothing is all right.'

To begin with, she'd sent Kira away with a being that seriously encroached the limits of Blake's realm of acceptability.

Now Level eleven was under emergency power after the Final Meld had released an energy surge large enough to register on the Richter scale. Not to mention one of the carapaces had torn an elevator shaft to shreds, thanks to a ludicrous embellishment she was entirely responsible for. Blake had given her metal angels wings— Telteriun wings— daydreaming of future military contracts that may evolve from her concept designs.

She was not going insane. She had arrived some time ago.

Cym closed the compartment door. A sickly pink gash marked his forehead, and burn marks covered one of his hands. But the damage was already half of what it had been when she'd rushed to his side in the level eleven chamber.

'How is Tamas?' Still leaning against the bed for support, Blake peered around Cym. The crowd had left Tamas's bedside. His face was cleaned of blood, revealing a disturbingly pale pallor. His skin tone dipped beneath its usual olive hue, the loss of blood draining the colour to a greyish-white. His broken wrist was strapped, and bandages covered the deep gash on his head. In light of the maelstrom he'd been at the centre of, he'd gotten off lightly.

'His blood pressure was extremely high, his respiratory rate accelerated, but that's been contained. The human surgeon will tend to his broken bone, and that will in time heal.' While Cym spoke, his eyes drifted not to Tamas but rather towards where Gren lay beneath his colourful halo. A flit of something – melancholy? – crossed his smooth, carved features. Blake straightened, fighting to recall where else she'd seen that exact expression.

'And Perry?' she said.

'He's kept alive only by those machines.' Cym returned his focus to the room. 'But I've been instructed to continue the life support. The captain hopes to gain further knowledge of what assailed the man. But that enquiry has — how do you say it? Taken a back seat?' He offered her a hesitant smile.

And it dawned on her — where she'd seen that look he'd given Gren. It had been on Eron's face when he'd seen Kira in the level eleven chamber that day she'd called them both to view Azrael. Blake bit the inside of her cheek. Was there no one but her in this forsaken place who was not absorbed in a ridiculous affair?

'Are they here, Cym?' Blake did not return the smile. 'I need to know.' She stopped herself from saying it was the least he could do. He may have assisted her with controlling the toxin in her blood, but he was also the one who'd made it possible for Tamas to carve the truth out of her with the serum. Every bitter inch of her terrible truth. 'Did they find Kira?'

Cym traced a steady finger over the sheet. His hesitation was momentary. 'She was not in Melgrove. The accommodation you spoke of had no new guests at all that day. The guests they were expecting, a Mr and Mrs Belvedere, did not show up.'

'Oh.' Blake leaned against the edge of the bed, swallowing against the lump at the back of her throat. Belvedere, Kira's favourite vodka. An pathetically emotive choice on Blake's part.

'But she is not safe.' Cym crossed his arms. 'There has been a murder—'

'Jesus.' Blake gasped. The ache bloomed wider, the hollowness reaching into her ribs.

'Not her,' Cym said. 'No. Kira is not deceased.'

'Bloody hell, Cym.'

'I apologise.' He raised his arms as though he meant to touch her, but decided against it. 'No. They believe that a death at a hotel in a place called Beleiro may have involved her. She was identified as being present, but there is no official record of her attending the hotel. Do you know anything about that, Blake?'

Blake did not make eye contact, uncertain that she was guarding her expression sufficiently. 'No, Cym. I do not. Use your serum again if you don't believe me. Go ahead .'

And she would rip the needle out of his hand and turn it on him. Strip his words from him and turn him inside out. The Syranian god-soldiers were expected to act like chaste eunuchs. If the captain learned of a relationship existing between them, his vehemence towards Kira and Eron would pale in comparison.

Cym pressed back, as though he sensed her rage. 'I did not wish to do that to you—'

'But you did.' Blake let go of the bed, forcing herself to take a breath and focus on the important details. Kira hadn't gone to Melgrove. As always, beautifully defiant. 'What happened at the hotel?' She gestured to Perry. 'Another ataku?'

'Utukku?' he said. 'There is no way of knowing. We have had no time to assess, and the body is in human custody. But the circumstances are certainly unusual.'

'Was Azrael with her?'

Rossiter was most certainly not. The time needed for him to travel across country simply didn't allow it. But she'd sent him to the right place. Kira had defied her, just as she hoped she would. Blake fought to keep her composure.

'It is believed so, though there is no actual footage. The gallu's presence seems to play havoc with surveillance equipment.'

Blake frowned. There had been some static on the footage from the Wheel and Barrow when she'd contacted Kira to advise her on the plan. But nothing that had made either of them indiscernible.

'Blake, is there some way you can reach her?' Cym edged in closer, voice lowered. Considerably taller than she was, he loomed over her.

'You must have heard my answer the first time you asked.' Blake raised her chin, holding his much-higher gaze. 'I screamed it after you injected me.'

His white eyes gave little away, but a muscle in his elongated neck twitched. 'And that pains me—'

'Not as much as it pained me.'

Cym glanced over his shoulder. Aside from one attendant still with Tamas, they were alone on the ward. 'Blake, if there is any way you can think of to contact Kira, you must do it. They mean to retrieve Azrael at any cost. The longer this goes on, the less patience the captain has.'

'They have four completed carapaces down there. I don't think Nex is obsessing over Azrael.'

'No. He is not the one obsessing. Our Lord is. The goddess even more so. You may discount our gods, but I can assure you their furies are very real. Ereshkigal wants Azrael back. You must find a way. The gods do not tolerate their rules being flouted.' Stretching his long arms, he placed his hands gently over hers and stilled the violent trembling.

Blake's immediate reaction was to pull away. To place some distance between them. Even at the best of times, the close proximity would bother her. But she wanted him to hurt. Even if it was just a little. She shifted closer to the Syranian.

'We don't always get what we want. Do we, Cym? I see your secret, without having to torture it from you. Do you think the captain would like to know,' she jerked her head towards Gren, 'that Eron isn't the only disgusting, weak, embarrassment among you?'

If she'd had any doubt, it was gone now. The Syranian lips pressed, as though fighting an urge to vomit. His white eyes scanned the air between them.

'No . . . it is not . . .'

But it was. And they both knew it. Blake's attempt to antagonise the Syranian, a childish thing in the scheme of things, had hit harder than she'd anticipated. Cym's distress was evident. She'd sliced into something raw and painful. And was none too proud of it.

Cym lifted his hands from hers. 'Blake, I will not forgive myself for what I did to you. So I cannot expect it of you. It has been an honour to work at your side. Whatever else I may be forced to do, I will not desert my attempts to find a cure for your contamination. Go.' He pulled a small vile from a pocket on his fitted coat. A wrapped syringe followed. Blake would have stepped back, but she was already pressed up against the edge of the bed. 'This is a lighter dose of the medication I gave you at your apartment. I can see that your symptoms have re-emerged, with renewed strength.' His eyes dropped to her hands. Shaking with all the fervour of a Parkinson's victim. 'Take this as my plea for forgiveness. And know that I only try to help you. But you must understand, this battle is not one you can win.'

Kira - 22

Fugitives need to sleep. That was Leona's decree. Everyone was running on empty, and sleepy people made shit decisions. Considering they were based several towns away from Beleiro, in a house that held no connection whatsoever to Kira or the Facility, and that the Rudiment they were supposedly going to find nirvana in was at least four hours' drive away, getting shut-eye hadn't seemed a bad idea. So that's what they had done. Kira had been certain there would be no way she'd sleep. Despite the copious amounts of wine.

Wrong. Even on the rock-hard mattress, she'd slept like a baby. Assuming babies slept so deeply not even dreams could seep into the darkness.

For four fucking hours. What kind of dumb-ass wanted-for-murder suspects lay spread-eagled in a bed, snoring their hearts out for that long?

So now here they were, on the road at three in the morning, travelling along the wide-open highway at the heart-stopping rate of a snail on Mary Jane. Leona seemed to go out of her way to find the potholes, crunching the poor bloody car through a maze of them. Azrael sat beside her. He and Vail were playing the world's most irritating game of 'name that random thing'. The kid was pointing out targets, asking Azrael if he knew what they were; the answer was always no. Vail would then launch into excruciating detail about everything from gas stations to streetlights and Az's reaction was always the same: smooth-faced nothingness.

Kira shifted her butt, trying to avoid the crack in the vinyl seat. Someone was going to get a slap soon if the game didn't stop. She wasn't in the friggin' mood. The tablet balanced on her knees, the Skyler messaging screen open and waiting. The kid was nothing if not prepared. Vail's phone was fucked after the casino debacle, but he'd hooked into a mobile hotspot somehow, and the whole damn interweb sat in her lap. Three calls to Perry had gone unanswered. He was showing 'offline', but he never set it to 'available', so that meant nothing. She had tried the Wheel and Barrow before she'd left the house. There had been no answer. Place must have been pumping, busiest night of the week and all. Music too loud to hear the call. After all, what self-respecting publican was hanging out in the back office?

'That your sister you're calling?' Leona watched her in the rearview mirror.

Kira scowled at her. 'No. It isn't. You're the one harping on about it being a dumb idea to call her.' *Don't push it witchy. Really not the moment.*

'Maiden's laces, girl, I don't believe for a second you'll pay any attention to what I have to say. Who is it then?'

'Easter bunny.'

'Easter bunny know anything about what's going on at the Facility?'

'He didn't answer. Busy making more fucking bunnies.' Kira rapped her metal fingers against the screen. At least the inane game had stopped. But why the hell did everyone feel the need to stare at her? Goddamn this car was far too bloody crowded.

'How about the internet?' Vail said. Bradley sat on his shoulder, goggle-eyed and gross. 'Are there any more reports about what happened?'

'You asked me that ten minutes ago.' Bitchy Kira smacked one out of the park and lined up for a second. 'Jesus, you can read. You do it.'

She thrust the tablet at him. Vail and Bradley blinked in unison.

'Kira, is everything –'

'Everything is just fucking dandy. Thanks for asking. Take it. Your Smoking Gun geeks are the only site harping about anything.'

She'd found one badly lit video filmed from out in the desert, way back from the Facility itself. The guy holding the phone camera rushed the image back and forth between his buddy in the driver's seat – a redhead with one of those massive round earrings that stretched your lobes to kingdom come – and a blur of yellow light in the distance that he assured anyone idiotic enough to be watching was the Facility. Hello Kitty dangled from the rearview mirror, mildly amused.

The only other snippet she'd found was from the local news station in Pryden. A small article, nothing too fanfare-ish, but no surprises there; the editor was most likely tucked into the Facility's deep pockets. There had been reports of an explosion, but the Facility was refusing to comment when contacted. Also no surprises.

If Az didn't stop batting those demon-lord-emerald dewdrops at her, she was going to hit him.

'I'm sure she's all right.' Leona still watched her, and the car drifted into the next lane.

'Watch the bloody road.'

Leona's jerk on the wheel was way too dramatic for the level of imminent danger they were in. Which was none. On the long stretch of liquorice ahead of them, they were the only car in sight.

'What has crawled into your britches, young lady?'

'Nothing. Nothing at all. That's the fucking problem.'

It had hit her as she'd tried to call Perry on Skyler. Blake wasn't on any messenger apps. She only had her cell phone.

'Oh for goodness sake,' Leona said. 'This trip will be unbearable if you're going to sulk the whole way. Just call your sister—'

Oh, bad move, Tan Queen. 'I can't.' Kira punched the back of Leona's seat. Using her metal fist. Making sure it made a dent. 'I don't know her fucking number.'

Goddamn, that had been louder than intended. Az reached for her just as Leona jammed on the brakes, and his hand swung wide. Everyone in the car jolted forward, and Kira winced as the seat belt jabbed the bruising on her shoulder.

'Jesus, what are you doing?' she said.

'Stopping until you calm down.' Leona declared, pulling on the handbrake. 'You don't know your own sister's number?'

Vail shook his head. 'Leona, you don't need to sound so disgusted. If you had a cell phone, you'd get it. The numbers are all stored—'

'We're in the middle of the highway, you crazy cow.' Kira peered out through the streak-stained back window. Not even a distant speck of an oncoming car. But still.

Leona jerked her head, butterfly clips fluttering almost like the real thing. 'I'm neither crazy nor a cow. But now at least I understand why you are acting so dreadfully. May I suggest that you take up meditation when you next have a chance?'

Kira leaned forward, not proud of the fact that Vail edged back when she did so, but the queen of the super-tan was way out of line. 'May I suggest that you start the bloody car and keep driving?'

Leona wasn't good with following orders. The car remained stationery. 'Adults talk through their feelings, Kira. If you are afraid for your sister, just say so. You have every right to be. She has involved herself, and you, in something far beyond her.'

'Leona.' Vail put his hand on her shoulder, and Bradley chirruped. 'Let it go. I think she gets the gist.' He turned his attention to Kira. 'Do you remember any numbers at all, anyone else you could contact, who might know?'

There was one number she remembered. It was stuck in her head like it had been branded there. But dead men don't answer phones. Hell, batteries went pretty damn flat after three years. 'No. I don't.'

It often felt like she and Blake were on different planets. Now they may as well be. Might as well be in that Kur place where Az and the big-titted goddess hung out.

'When we get to the Rudiment, maybe William can help you with memory recall.' Leona's tone reeked of trying-too-hard-to-be-nice. 'There are ways to –'

'I'm not getting bloody hypnotised by some cult leader. Can you please just drive, Leona? How much further have we got to go?'

Rain began to fall, a light drizzle. Leona pushed the car into gear and flicked on the windscreen wipers. They wailed like banshees across the glass. Az traced his finger down the window, following a bead of water.

'An hour and a bit.' Vail's voice lifted with false enthusiasm. As if everyone were perfectly okay with being crammed in the shitbox a bit longer. 'Nearly there.'

Bullshit, but Kira had done enough tantrum-throwing for five minutes. The car started rolling again. Azrael used both hands to trace raindrop patterns. Very demonic. Kira returned her attention to the tablet. Distraction would be good. Maybe one of the stupid-ass stories the poor old Sumerians made up. Vail had downloaded a few before they'd left the house. She picked one called 'Inanna's Descent to the Underworld'. Sounded porn centric, so it would do.

Turns out Ereshkigal had had a big falling out with her sister, some other scantily clad chick called Inanna, a goddess of war and love and fertility. Inanna had passed through seven gates to get to Kur, taking off her clothes as she went till she'd arrived at her sister's throne, stark naked and acting all innocent. *No, no dear sister, I haven't come to take your throne. Flutter eyes.*

Jesus, now there was a god Kira wanted to be. Queen of sex, violence, and giving her sister a fucking hard time. But there'd be a name change. Inanna sucked.

All at once the cabin brightened, and the guttural sound of an engine filled the damp air.

'This bloody idiot is absolutely flying.' Leona screwed up her face, eyes darting back and forth from rearview mirror to road.

'Police?' Kira's empty stomach dipped. She turned around, gripping the back of the seat.

'Not unless police drive luxury cars in this part of the world,' Leona said.

True to the witch's word, there was something a little bit fancy behind them. Kira squinted into the lights and caught sight of a wide-mouth grill and trident logo. Maserati. Silver. Nice. She'd driven one herself a couple of times. Hooked up with a girl in New York who drove a mauve one. Disgusting colour. Impressive car.

Despite the fact that the driver had three lanes of highway to choose from, they apparently liked the ass end of Leona's powder-blue shitbox.

'For crying out loud,' Leona muttered, 'go around.'

Kira settled back into her seat. Even the creepazoid lizard wanted a look. He perched on the front bench seat, flicking his candy-floss tongue in the general direction of the pushy driver. But Az sat still, head tilted down, eyes shadowed. Sleeping? Or had his batteries run out? She laid her hand on his arm, just as the Maserati overtook them. One subtle press of the accelerator and the driver could be in the next state over before the Datsun's wheels made another rotation. But the driver slowed alongside, and the window slid open.

A woman. Dark hair down to her shoulders, the dimness of the interior distorting her features. She glanced over at them as she eased the car past. She didn't seem to be in too much of a hurry now. Leona wound down her window.

'Do you have a problem?' she shouted.

The rain spattered in through the open window, straight into Kira's face. Mildly refreshing.

'What's she saying?' Vail said.

Leona didn't answer, and Kira could hear the very faint murmur of the woman speaking. She couldn't make out a single word over the grumble of the Maserati and the gush of the wind, but Leona seemed to get the gist.

'No idea. Sorry, love,' she said, winding up her window.

Kira wiped at her damp face. 'What did she want?'

'Directions to some place I've never heard of.' Leona shrugged. 'I'm not exactly a local.'

'Weird, I would have thought a car like that would have GPS.' Vail said.

Bradley broke out one of those mini chihuahua barks, clearly directing his yelps at Azrael. The guy still sat with his head lowered and his fingers held in stiff claws. Rocking. Ever so slightly.

Oh, shit. Not good.

'Az? Hey, buddy.' Kira didn't move to touch him. Didn't move at all. She'd learned sitting with him at the Facility that when he got like this, sinking into what sure as hell looked like a panic attack, that any sudden movement would have him thrashing about like a madman. So would the dark. The dude hated the dark. Hell, not even dark, just badly lit and he went total unhappy camper. Azrael lifted his hands, clutched at his head. Maybe the interior of the car was getting to him. Dim and gloomy.

'You need to pull over,' Kira said. 'Now.'

For the first time since bolting from the hotel, she realised the tranq bracelet was still sitting beside the sink in the bathroom. Christ almighty. Exhibit A of 'Kira was here'. Police had probably traced it back to the Facility by now. A throaty sound escaped Az, and the rocking amped up enough to make the seat shudder.

'What's happening?' Leona said.

He'd been behind thick glass every time Kira had seen him lose it since her very first run in with him. Her ribcage still bore the brunt of that introduction, and they didn't have Eron to keep Az from tearing this bucket of bolts to pieces if he lost it again.

'Stop the fucking car.' Kira chewed each word slowly.

'Kira said we need to stop.' Vail was old-man calm. 'Over there on the left, Leona. It's a rest stop. Quickly, we need to pull over.'

Azrael slammed his hands against the window, clawing at the glass as though he wanted to scratch the raindrops out of existence. Leona didn't skimp on the quickly part of Vail's direction, swerving the car hard left.

'Hey, buddy, come on,' Kira said. 'Az, we know how to deal with this, right? Just look at me.'

He swiped at his seat belt, snapping it like a piece of cotton thread. He did manage to look at her, just for a moment. Then his head snapped forward, as if he couldn't hold any part of himself still for too long. He lashed out, slamming his hand into the back of the seat. The entire bench seat hopped, bolts squealing.

'Bloody hell!' Leona cried.

'Az, please just hold it together.' Kira's hands fluttered, useless. She couldn't touch him, but it was all she wanted to do. 'Just hold on. You're safe. I've got you.'

Leona floored it, and the powder-blue pile of crap revved into the stratosphere. The gear box screamed for a change as Leona drove them into the rest stop.

'Under that light over there, we need somewhere really bright.' Kira pointed towards a spotlight illuminating a billboard. 'Park with the headlights pointing towards the board, and get them on high beam.'

Bright as all hell. That's the only way you dragged someone out of the darkness. You annihilated it. For the second time in as many minutes, Leona did exactly as she was told. The moment the car slowed, Kira jumped out.

'Anything I can do to help?' Vail called.

'Just stay out of arm's reach.'

Az threw himself up against his door before Kira could reach it. It flew open with a screech of metal and unhappy hinges. Azrael tumbled out, a mess of hurried limbs. He fell to his knees, a godawful sound wrenching from him.

'Az, hey, let's just focus here, okay?' Kira kept her distance. 'You are okay. See the light? And we're all friends. You're okay, Az. Listen to me.'

He got to his feet. Clearly not okay. The mother of all fucking meltdowns was happening, and Kira had no clue why. There were no Syranian asshats treating him like a steer at a rodeo. The light from the sign lit his face almost as well as the sun would have. Usually just getting in his line of sight slowed things down a little, as if he used her as an anchor to focus on and pull himself out of whatever dark place he was in. But it wasn't working here. And she'd put money on him bolting any second. So Kira did the only thing she could think of. She took his hand, her metal hand grabbing for his equally false one. Contact was a mule kick. A jolt as if she'd touched an electric fence. She gritted her teeth and held on. Tried to reach him. All her muscles clenched, but not in a *I'm-about-to-cum* kind of way. Not even close. The sensation felt biting and coarse against her nerves. The dude was sinking into some bad mojo. Kira closed her eyes, and Azrael shifted in her grip. She needed something to hold on to here, mentally hold on to. Picture something cute. Sweet. Not scary.

Puppies. Always a good start. Piglets. Another winner. Puppies and piglets playing together. In the snow. Jackpot.

The sizzle edged down into something more comfortable. Warmer. And the fear dissolved. Less held-hostage-and-tortured kind of terror, more watching-a-scary-movie-with-your-buddies.

'Kira.' Azrael breathed her name.

She opened her eyes. They both stood very still. His disjointed swaying had stopped. Azrael's eyelids were low, but he was looking right at her. Not through her.

'Az. Glad you're back.' Where the fuck had he gone? She had dark times, but Christ on a cracker, this had been next level.

Kira took a step backwards, still holding tight. When Azrael moved with her, she continued until they were both in front of the car, soaked in the bright light of the headlights. The shitbox had impressive high beams. She squinted. The tension left Azrael, his shoulders sinking, posture slumping. He tilted his head back, looking directly into the glow of the advertisement that declared everyone needed more Metamucil in their lives.

Kira took a steadying breath. Now the sensation was much more like the first time, the part where muscles melted and everything went gooey and delicious.

'That really was most impressive.'

Kira blinked against the glare, peering in the direction of the voice somewhere over her right shoulder. Azrael pulled his hand from hers, a sudden tug that made her think for a second he'd fallen over. The car headlights switched off, and the engine gurgled into silence.

'Who is that?' Kira's vision was filled with blobs of yellow. 'Leona? Vail?'

'It is not them,' Azrael said, all bunched up and tense again.

She'd known it wasn't Vail or Leona, but had kinda hoped one of them would call out anyway.

'Oh they are fine,' the speaker said. There was an accent there, English definitely but something else Kira couldn't pinpoint. Unquestionably female. 'They may have headaches when they wake up but will be totally fine. I would send my sincere apologies, but that would be insincere. I tried the whole Wiccan thing once upon a time, but they are truly irritating with all their nature-loving, stinking-herb rubbish.'

Azrael threw his arm across Kira's stomach and shoved her in behind him, his arms splayed out just enough to let her know she wasn't going anywhere.

'What are you doing?' she hissed.

'It is the same,' he said, his voice lower and more growly than she'd heard before. 'It is the same as before.'

He shook his head, a violent jerk back and forth. She half expected him to slam his fists against his temple.

'This is what freaked you out?' Kira whispered.

'Well, it was rather unexpected for me, too, I have to say.' The speaker stepped into the light – and Kira's first stupid random thought was *nice coat*. That thought was followed by *Holy shit, it's that chick from the Maserati*. She didn't look particularly dangerous or freak-out inducing, unless you found killer wardrobes threatening. Az wasn't making it easy to take a good look at her, though, edging back and forth like a goalie in a soccer game. He clearly didn't want Kira to go anywhere near the woman, but that didn't stop her from approaching them. She was sleek grace on high black heels. The white knee-length coat she wore moved with an ease that suggested the same luxury as the car. The collar was turned up, accentuating the woman's long neck and dark features: dark eyes, and long, snaking raven curls playing at the base of her honey-kissed throat. Her purple wrap dress highlighted the curve of her hips and the bulge of her breasts. All in all, she was fucking hot. Kira frowned. And very familiar.

'Do you really want me to leave?' The woman drew closer, and Azrael's tension levels started to re-boil. He was rigid, like a pole had been shoved up his ass. 'Surely you are as curious as I am, beautiful boy.'

She spoke in a low, husky tone, rich with invitation and suggestion. And that's when full recall hit. Kira knew this woman. *Really* knew this woman. She'd traipsed around her mound of Venus more than once. In Greece, eons ago. It had been quite the party. Quite the week. Kira knew exactly what those boobs looked like. Felt like. The hair had been very different, though, short then and snow white, and her skin darker after long days spent naked beside an impossibly azure ocean.

'Oh my god,' Kira breathed.

Azrael turned at her voice, and the woman walked right up to him and reached a slender arm to touch his chest. Both the woman and Azrael cried out. Hers was a sound of pleasure, but Azrael screamed, an anguished, hollow sound. A gut-wrenching sound Kira'd heard too many times at the Facility.

Kira ducked under Az's raised arm and went in for the rugby tackle before she had time to think it through.

'Back off!' she shouted.

The impact knocked the wind out of her but it worked. As Kira hit the ground with a grunt, the woman tumbled with her. The world was all white for a moment as they scuffled, then Kira managed to throw a leg over, her knees digging the edges of the white coat into the asphalt. If nothing else, the woman would need a dry cleaner. Little grunts and huffs of effort followed before Kira got a hold of the woman's narrow wrists and found herself in a very familiar position – straddling a lusciously curved body, leaning forward to press the woman's hands up over her head. Their faces close. The woman took deep breaths, her breasts moving up and down in distracting waves. Kira tried to keep her focus on the rich brown eyes gazing up at her from beneath arched black brows.

'I know you,' Kira said. Her body maybe, but not her name. Kira felt the memory surge forward, blurry and slippery. Something that started with N.

'You do. Very well.' Thick, long lashes lowered, her gaze fixing on something over Kira's shoulder. 'Where did you find him?'

'Who are you?'

The woman widened her almond eyes in mock surprise. 'I'm deeply offended, Kira. I thought I was more than a notch on the bedpost.'

'Nina . . .' Bingo. Thanks brain. 'It's Nina.'

There was another sound, like metal across a sharpening stone, and the woman gasped. Kira risked a glance over her shoulder.

'What the sweet fucking Jesus is happening?' she cried.

Azrael had wings. Proper fucking wings, like someone had taken them from a gargantuan eagle and dipped them in matte silver paint and strapped them to his back. Their appearance seemed to be as much of a surprise to him as to anyone else. Azrael jerked, left and right, trying to peer over his shoulders. The wings themselves were massive, easily his height in length and as wide as surfboards, and clearly he had no idea what to do with them. The tip of the right wing hit the asphalt, raking across it, sending a small spray of sparks and stone into the air. Though they might have been shaped and marked like feathers, it was safe to say the wings weren't made of anything light and soft. More like knife blades. And Azrael was no sushi chef. He stumbled. Kira flung herself off the woman, barely managing to lie flat before the left wing sliced through the air above her.

'Az, stop moving!' she shouted.

But the weight of the appendages left him chaotically unbalanced. He went down on one knee, and the left wing tip dipped. It speared into the pavement and lodged there. The woman, Nina, took the opportunity to push herself to her feet, dusting off the now not-so-white coat.

'He is magnificent.' She laughed. 'But this cannot be. He is impossible. Tell me his name.'

When Kira didn't answer straight away, the woman turned to face her. Her cheeks glistened. Tears. Weird. She hadn't seemed like the emotional type, in Greece or here. Kira's answer, though, would have to wait. Azrael jerked his shoulder, and the wing tip tore free of the ground. The release threw him sideways, and the long, curving segments that made up the right wing bit through the air like a horizontal guillotine.

'Move!' Kira launched herself at Nina. Down they went. This was getting to be a habit. Kira glanced up in time to see the wing headed straight for her. She threw her metal arm up into the air, and the impact lifted her off the ground before dumping her back down and rolling her across the gravel. 'Shit, bugger, shit.'

The skin on her flesh arm was peppered with scrapes. Showering was going to suck. Kira rolled onto her back, grimacing. Metal arm still intact. Good thing. Head still on. Even better.

'Kira, have I hurt you?' Azrael crouched down next to her, and, despite herself, Kira shrank back.

Her answer was *Hell yes, that fucking hurt*, but she couldn't bring herself to say it. Maybe she had a little concussion, too, because the way he knelt over her, with the light behind him, framing his silhouette, took her breath away. Then it hit her. The silhouette was sans wings. 'Dude, where did they go?'

He shuffled in a half circle, like a puppy trying to see its own tail. Kira gagged. His back was a pulpy, bloody mess, shirt fabric ripped to shreds, faux skin likewise. The deep gashes gave her a clear view of the metal glinting between his shoulder blades. 'Jesus, that's gross.'

Wings. What shit was Blake snorting down there? Azrael offered her his hand, and she took it, letting him pull her to her feet. He didn't let go, his focus on her metal limb, turning it this way and that as he looked for damage. Handling her as if she were a baby bird.

'Okay.' Kira pulled her hand away. 'I'm all good. Where the hell is that chick?'

'There is blood.' Azrael touched a finger to her right cheek. 'I have hurt you.'

'It wasn't you, it was the pavement.' He needed to stop with the puppy-dog eyes and focus. 'Az, where did that woman go?'

She was definitely not where Kira had left her on the ground. Somehow a woman in a white ankle-length coat and heels straight off the runway had managed to slip away.

'Okay, Az, get in the car.' Kira pushed him towards the shitbox and found out her left hip hadn't done so well in the drop-and-roll adventure. 'Fuck me.'

'Kira?' A voice came from beyond the car. 'Are you guys okay?'

The kid. Vail stumbled out from behind the toilet block on the far side of the parking lot, Leona's arm was draped around his shoulder. She didn't look so flash, sagging against the kid.

'Where the hell have you been?' Kira shouted.

Leona raised her head but didn't let go of Vail. 'Unconscious. Is the bright one all right?'

Kira readied a snappy retort about how she'd nearly been decapitated, thanks for asking; then she caught sight of Azrael, and the reply died on her lips. The guy reminded her of Perry after she'd dragged him onto a roller coaster. Shell-shocked, not sure whether to vomit or cry. Perry had done both.

Azrael, though, did neither. He just gripped the roof of the car as though it was all that kept him on his feet.

'He's been better.'

Vail and Leona reached them. The kid cradled Bradley in his free hand, the little slimeball's sides inflating with each gulping, rapid breath he took. Nina had somehow just managed to put a big dent in all of them. Kira traced her fingers over the metalwork of her arm, searching for actual dents and scratches.

'That woman,' she said, 'was she one of your witchy friends?'

'No.' One of Leona's false eyelashes had fallen off, and her natural lashes were sparse and stunted. 'No, that was not one of ours.' She had to clear her throat to get the words clear. 'I've never seen anything like that.'

'Fucking great to know. All right.' Kira opened the passenger and back doors in quick succession, ignoring the painful tweak in her shoulder. 'Vail, you've got your learner's. Tell me you have your learner's, cause queen of the snails here is out.'

'Well, I have got it, but I don't know –'

Kira cursed her car-driving phobia for the first time in a long time. 'You'll drive over the speed limit, or I'll punch you in the dick. Deal?'

Vail sighed, not half as intimidated as she would have liked and Leona muttered about 'issues', but they all got in the car. Bowl-cut boy in the driver's seat.

Tamas - 23

Ereshkigal had not walked his dreams since the day Tamas
became an orphan. After all had been said and done and funeral
preparations had been underway, he'd slept deeply, as though he
were as dead as his mother. The goddess had visited his dream, in a
location just like this. Not much had been said, and if it had been,
he didn't recall the conversation. But he'd known he was being
assessed. Given the once-over. Whether she had been disappointed
or satisfied, he had no clue. But even the goddess had little choice

in the matter. He was her Messenger by birthright. Take it or leave it.

Tamas stood in the exact same desert he'd found himself in six years ago, watching her move towards him through the pale gold sand. A river wound through low sandhills beyond her, grasslands, like the one his mother had cultivated at the Facility, clinging to the banks. The dreamscape was the goddess's memory of the land she had once dominated.

Sumer.

He wondered if Ereshkigal would recognise any of it now. And whether she'd been disappointed when precognition had directed her to the other side of the globe to locate Dumuzi. His mother certainly had been. She'd hated the thought of moving to the States. But then, she'd hated a lot of things.

The child drew closer. Tamas preferred to avoid children and, therefore, could only take a wild guess at the age Ereshkigal had assumed. Ten maybe. Skin black as onyx, eyes just as dark. Hair short against her skull in tight natural curls. She wore a small wrap dress, blood red with gold trimming. Feet bare on the sand. Mirages shimmered in the distance behind her, suggesting the presence of heat, but he sensed no warmth, or coolness. Nor any sound or wind. It was like being stuck in a vivid painting. His own fearful anticipation was the most tangible thing about the place.

His last memory was of the Final Meld. The tremendous rush of energy catapulted up from Kur had been far, far greater than that at Azrael's arrival. At one point Tamas had feared his skull would crack and the skin peel from his flesh. Had he been successful? Had he died in the Meld? For all he knew, he was strewn in a million pieces now. Being trampled by those around him, already forgotten. He interlaced his fingers against the hollowness that found its way through the dreamscape. Was she coming to receive him into Kur or to tear him to shreds because he'd failed? Both, maybe? Impale him on hooks in her throne room, just as she'd done to her sister Inanna.

Eternal torture for making a mistake.

In the dream world, his panic didn't manifest as anything more than a distant ripple of unease, but he'd be screaming into his pillow in the real world.

Tamas waited. If he started towards her, he'd find himself chasing a mirage. Impossible to catch. Ereshkigal came in her own time. He glanced down, and dismay mingled with doubt. He was naked. All his bits exposed. A chest he'd never succeeded in bulking up, thighs too pear-shaped, too feminine. And a penis, mottled brown and stubby, so rarely used for anything but pissing he may as well have not had one at all.

The child reached him and stopped a couple of metres away. Eyes like black holes fixed on him. Diminutive in height, with chubby cheeks and tiny hands, Ereshkigal looked nothing like the image the Sumerian's had carved of her — a buxom woman with clawed feet, standing astride a pair of lions — but her presence was just as intimidating. It heated the air, the first hint of temperature he'd sensed.

'You are not dead.' Ereshkigal spoke in the high pitch of childhood. 'You will wake.'

A dream then. Tamas dropped to his knees, bowing his head momentarily to hide his relief before raising his eyes to meet hers.

'My lady, have I served you well?'

The child stood, statue-like, giving no hint of the goddess's state of mind. 'That remains undecided. The Four have ascended. This much is done. But you fail to return what was taken from me.'

Her eyes were ink black, and Tamas fought the urge to lean away. 'I have promised you, my lady, that Azrael will be found.' He paused, unease prickling his dream-sense. The goddess had been distant when he'd advised her of Azrael's disappearance, a sense of annoyance filling him as she'd danced about his skull. But distracted. Far more concerned with the state of the carapaces and his readiness to begin the Meld. This sudden focus, the hint of underlying rage, was a new development.

Ereshkigal toyed with the folds of her dress. 'Azrael is a false name. The one I sent to you is known as Enkidu. And if you do not wish to join in his damnation, then you will find him and return him to me.'

The shock of hearing the name raised Tamas's head. 'Enkidu? He lives?'

A wild man. Literally. Thousands of years ago when the gods had walked amongst the mortal on Earth, Enkidu had been birthed from the wildness of nature by the goddess of creation, and sent to teach benevolence to a powerful king who'd lost the support of his people. Historical records showed he'd done that and more, becoming the lover and constant companion of the great Sumerian king Gilgamesh. But the wild man was thought long dead. At the hands of the gods themselves.

'At my behest he lives. My brothers and sisters condemned him to death, but they failed to heed my protest at their decision. I will not be ignored. Death is not a great enough punishment for what Enkidu stole from me. In the darkness of Kur I have bound him. Taunted him.' The child kicked at the sand. 'Made his suffering unending. But I saw purpose for him, in this hunt for Dumuzi. Only the strongest could go before the Four, and truly test the restraints that awaited them.'

Tamas didn't dare move. Not even to blink. The story of Gilgamesh and Enkidu was one he knew by heart, as well as any Christian knew about Jesus. Under Enkidu's influence, Gilgamesh had become a hero to his people, slaying the supermundane creatures prevalent when the divine had walked the Earth. The king had protected his realm from monsters with the help of his wildman. And Gilgamesh's reputation had attracted the attention of the gods themselves. One in particular. The goddess Inanna, who wanted to reward him in a way only the goddess of fertility could do. But when Gilgamesh turned down her advances she had been enraged. The slight hadn't gone down well with any of the gods. And they'd sent the Bull of Heaven—the inspiration behind the constellation Tauras— to destroy both Gilgamesh and Enkidu.

But the Bull of Heaven had another name. Gugalanna. Husband to the goddess, Ereshkigal.

The child's head tilted, a hard, sharp move that would have broken an actual human neck. 'But Enkidu shall never have his freedom. His punishment for destroying what was mine, will not end. Lahar and his servants will tend to the Four. You will dedicate yourself to locating Enkidu and those who removed him. Show great discretion. The attention of my brethren would be most unwelcome. They must not learn of this. Do you understand, Messenger?'

The sand seeped up over Tamas's knees, the weight of his body pressing him down into the soft surface. His emotions may have been dulled, but his thoughts were not, and they were barely able to fathom what he'd been told. Azrael was Enkidu.

'I understand.'

Azrael was one-half of a pair who had turned the tables on the gods, and killed the divine assassin sent to destroy them. The consequences had been dire, and swift. And Enkidu had born the brunt of it. The ancient texts told of his suffering from disease— with Gilgamesh forced to watch, helpless to save his lover—

enduring terrible pain for long and terrible months, before, finally, dying.

But the writings had been wrong about one thing at least. Enkidu was not dead.

Tamas's unease lurked, distant and subtle. Azrael was not some nameless gallu.

He was a god slayer.

Sand whipped against him, and the numbness of the dreamscape disappeared. Minute grains bit and scratched at every centimetre of his exposed skin. Pain shot across his groin, and he doubled over. The child lifted her hands and flung something at him. A spray of desert sand. He flinched, but before it reached him, the pellets gathered into a greater swirl. A humanoid figure began to form out of the maelstrom. It radiated warmth, a fledgling fire gathering strength. The specks tightened and solidified into something discernible. Azrael. On his knees, bent backwards by the force of the mea stones the Syranians used to control him. It was one of the many memories the goddess had syphoned from Tamas's mind each Calling. The wind churned harder, buffeting against him, seeming to want to throw him onto his back.

'Take these utukku I gift you. Use them wisely and hunt down my prey.' The child still stood with hands raised, and the sand-Azrael shattered into a million tiny pieces, circling in a pool at her feet, then reforming once again. This time Blake's image filled the space between Tamas and his mistress. She leaned over a half-constructed carapace, a skeleton of metal, bare of skin or features. 'Your Technician took what does not belong to her. Now she will endure the consequences. Take my blade, inflict it upon her mortal flesh, and she will languish as Enkidu did upon his mortal death bed. But death will be hers to enjoy only once the wildman is returned to us, there may be need of her yet.'

With a dismissive jerk of Ereshkigal's hand, the image of Blake exploded into tiny pellets. They swarmed at Tamas, landing with a force that threw him onto his back. The grains embedded themselves into his skin and began to burrow deeper, pushing him beneath the sand. He was sinking, melting, he did not know which. Particles crammed Tamas's mouth, and searing pain filled his tongue as the sand transformed to glass. He sank further, till only his eyes and nose met the air. Ereshkigal watched him, her human face devoid of any sentiment. Watching as his body, each cell, filled with the seething force spilling into him.

Tamas was returning. Back to the land of the living. And he was not going alone.

Kira - 24

Leona's 'safe house' was perched on top of a hill. A rundown colonial with wide verandas a few kilometres out of a one-street town called Jackson. The Datsun had rattled up the curving road, the engine straining against the slope. No chance of sneaking up on the occupants. The next town over would have heard their arrival, the sound of the dying car echoing across the open paddocks and fields that stretched as far as the eye could see in the predawn light.

She slapped at her arm, ending the action-packed life of the mosquito feasting on her blood. Crimson smeared the site of the insect's demise. Now it was so damn quiet here, Kira was pretty certain she could hear the hum of her mechanical heart. The grass was damp and cool against Kira's faux leather-clad butt. There were probably a million more comfortable places to sit inside the house, but she wasn't in the mood for indoors. Fresh air, that was the ticket. After hours in the shitbox, space and fresh air were high on the list of wants.

'Shit.' Another two mosquitoes died on her arm.

Actually, the outdoors sucked, but not as much as meet-and-greets. Normally, Kira was queen of the chat-with-people-you-don't-know circuit. Not today. Couldn't be fucked. Brain too full. Car too small. Fucking lizard too damn starey. The minute they'd pulled up outside the house, Kira'd mumbled about getting some space and headed across the lawn down towards where a paddock fence marked the start of the horseshit zone. Az had followed after her like the wing-wielding puppy that it turns out he was. And Vail had done his diplomacy thing again, ushering Leona inside, telling her to give them space. A couple of people had come out to greet them, but they'd been backlit by internal lights, and Kira hadn't made out any details.

She rubbed her eyes, knowing she should sleep or eat or do something normal. Certain she couldn't. On the weirdness scale, her life was up there. She watched Azrael, standing by a seen-better-days timber fence. She hadn't realised how much horses and their shit could stink, but he didn't seem to care. He held out a fistful of grass, an offering that the shit machines had been steadfastly ignoring for a good fifteen minutes now.

'Pretty sure you're not going to make a new best friend anytime soon.' Gotta give the guy points for persistence. She narrowed her eyes, spotting movement on the fence railing beside him. 'Oh great, you're here too. Yay for me.'

Bradley the wanna-be ninja, had followed them and now sat on the wood next to his new best buddy, a blob of black in the dull light. The sun set the distant mountains aglow. Any time now the harsh light of day would spill into the valley.

'You said they like grass.' Azrael punctuated each word as if pinning it to a corkboard.

'I know jack shit about horses. Maybe it's you, your demon blood is freaking them out.'

Azrael stepped back, quick, like the fence had zapped him. Bradley let out a little bark. Maybe she was going nuts, highly likely, but the little streak of black and orange sounded disapproving.

'Oh Jesus, chill out,' she said. 'Maybe horses are just dumb.'

Azrael released his clutch of grass, watching it fall to the ground in fluttering strips, and kept staring long after the last piece made landfall.

'It's grass, Az,' Kira said. 'And not the good kind.'

Crickets. Literally. Tough crowd. Apparently a sulky crowd. Azrael plonked himself down beside his fallen green soldiers and didn't turn when she called his name. Whatever. He wasn't the only one cracking the shits. She dug the tips of her metal fingers into the dirt, the sensors in the fingertips letting her know the soil was cold to the touch.

Cold was good. Might clear her head faster. Nina turning up had just blasted whatever sense Kira could make of all this out of the water. Before that, she could blame all this shit on Blake and that fucking weirdo Tamas, messing with aliens. In all the years she'd known him, Tamas and Kira had barely said ten words. The guy had all the money in the world, but that hadn't bought him a personality. A creepy, stuttering dude who never looked Kira in the eye.

The Facility had always been a weird-ass place. So weird-ass shit could happen, right? But Nina? A random – granted, *amazing* – fuck from a year ago appears in the middle of the night, looking as if she'd seen god when Azrael burst the wings out.

'Am I the only dickhead in the world who doesn't know what's going on?' Kira groaned.

A low chuckle, then, 'Highly unlikely.'

She jerked upright, a muscle in her neck spasming with the effort. 'Jesus Christ –'

'No, it's just me, I'm afraid. William.'

A kaftan-clad man emerged from the drooping branches of a weeping willow, flashlight in hand. Az didn't shift from his cross-legged lump of self-pity, keeping a cautious eye on their guest, but as calm as Az seemed to get. Which was good. Impaling random people seemed a bad idea. Bradley perched on Azrael's knee, head raised, tongue flicking.

'Welcome to my Rudiment.' William said, all up-beat and fucking annoying. 'I hope you'll come inside and check it out at some point. Do you mind if I join you? Azrael, would that be okay?'

Az didn't give two shits. Already back to looking at the horses.

'You're asking the guy who doesn't know what planet he's on.' Kira got to her feet.

The man laughed as if Kira were actually funny. It was a pity his name was William because he looked a hell of a lot like Santa Claus. The resemblance was admittedly vague in the costuming department – with the paisley green kaftan – but the belly, the pepper beard, and the full cheeks were right on point.

'Well, I hope I didn't startle you too much,' he said.

But Kira was too busy staring at the guy's torch to answer.

'Kira?'

'Tell me that's a bunch of fireflies.'

A ball of light hovered in the air just below his left hand, illuminating the ground before him.

'Oh, these guys? Yes, of course.' He smiled at her through the mellow-yellow glow. 'The Maiden we worship is of nature. Nature itself perhaps. And she strengthens our bond with the life you see around you. They are very pretty, don't you think?'

He lifted his hand, and the compact ball of light sprayed out into a hundred tiny sparks. The fireflies flitted in the air around him, but they didn't move away or dart off on whatever crazy mission most fireflies seemed to be on. They just hung there. Like glowing raindrops suspended in the air.

Kira wasn't about to tell him it was probably the most beautiful thing she'd ever seen. Impossible beauty in an ugly-ass world.

'You can't afford batteries?' she said.

Suddenly, the bugs decided shift was over. They lifted in unison, dashing high into the air, scattering in a hundred different directions. William uttered a surprised gasp, just as Kira sensed someone beside her. Azrael had left his four-footed friends and stood super close, staring up at the dispersing fireflies as specks of light blinked against the pink-frosted sky.

'They do not like me, either,' he said, all soppy, like a kid whose favourite teddy just spat on him.

Kira raised her metal hand to touch him, quickly swapping to her flesh hand before contact sent them both loopy-la-la again. But her own reaction caught her off guard. Consolation wasn't her thing. She lowered her arm.

'No, no, Azrael.' William clasped his hands together, his kaftan billowing with the movement. 'It is quite the opposite. They just haven't seen . . .' Kira glanced at him as the pause lengthened. William gave her a lopsided smile. 'Well, the sun is starting to rise. They realise they are not needed anymore.'

She had no idea why he was lying, but he was. Az had just scared the bugs stupid; they'd scattered like seals being chased by an orca. Even Azrael appeared unconvinced. He did a three-way dubious-look thing, between the sky, Kira, and William.

'Here, come Azrael.' William beckoned him towards the fence. 'You wanted to feed the horses, right? Well come, let me show you.'

He stood at the fence and stared out at the horses. Didn't make a sound, didn't do any strange summoning ritual, just stood there. The next minute three of the shit machines galloped towards the fence, all tossed manes and back-kicks to the air. Kira edged away, certain the damn things were going to clear the fence.

They didn't.

Once they reached the timber railings, they came to a snorting stop. William muttered something to them. Must have been telling them not to be scared of the demon, because a second later Azrael reached for the nearest one, a butt-ugly mottled brown-and-white lump, and it didn't move away. William told Azrael not to be frightened. Bradley, the ever-present reptile, was hitching a ride on Az's shoulder, and got sniffed over by the smallest of the horses, a brown thing that seemed to be deciding if the lizard was edible or not. But for the most part, Kira's attention focused on Az. He stood with his ass kind of poking back, his body taut, holding himself like a runner about to bolt off in the opposite direction, or shit himself. Finally, he laid a tentative hand on the horse's nose. The animal made a sound, a snort, tossed its head, and there was more muttering from William. Azrael ran his hand slowly up and down the long face. He turned towards her, and though he didn't smile, Kira knew he was having kittens. The dude was practically busting out of his metal shell.

She could feel it.

What the fuck? Kira thumped down on the grass, the impact sending an ache halfway up her spine. She pressed the heels of her palms into her eyes, conscious she was pressing too hard with her metal hand.

'Would you like one?'

She blinked against the spots filling her vision. William stood over her, holding out something. Small, white, and instantly recognisable.

'You're offering me a joint?' Kira said.

Maybe there was a god or two.

'Yes. Vail seemed to think you wouldn't be averse to it.'

'Oh, did he now? How progressive of him. What kind of a bloody coven is this, exactly?'

He laughed that frustratingly pleasant-sounding laugh again and lit the joint before answering. The scent hit her. Lush and rich and fucking fantastic.

'It's not a coven; there are no eyes of newt on the breakfast menu here. Though it is vegetarian, so I hope you don't mind.' He took a long, slow drag, letting the white vapour escape through his nose. 'Wicca, witches, wizards, pagans, the human race does love a label. But we are all simply servants of the Maiden. The power behind the glory that surrounds us.'

Seeing William inhale and stay upright, Kira decided the coast was clear. When he offered her the joint, she took it. Filled her lungs with one giant puff of heaven. It was good. Really, really good. And this was a bad, bad idea. She needed to be focused. Azrael remained in petting-zoo heaven for now, the horses moving in to cop a feel, but who knew what might trigger a wing burst?

Fuck it. She took another long drag. 'The Maiden?' she said. 'Okay, so it's some kind of sex cult then?'

Another one of these and she might be into it. A good session would make all this bearable. But Kira coughed on the thought of getting dirty with Leona. Nightmare territory.

'No. It is not a sex cult,' William said, indulgent and not even remotely patronising. Damn this guy. 'Though, sex being a natural energy, it is part of it all. But no orgies. I can assure you.'

'Boring.' Kira smiled a lazy green smile.

He sat down on the ground beside her, far enough away that it was comfortable, close enough that she didn't feel like a leper. Maybe if she asked nicely, they could just stay here, in this moment. Please Santa, this Christmas I'd like a moment frozen in time. Kira's smile etched up a notch. Her thoughts were so cute she wanted to cuddle them.

'Wouldn't boring be nice? I hear you've been through quite a lot the past few days.' He paused, and through her narrowed gaze, Kira noticed his eyes drop to her metal limb. 'So many things you've been through, and yet your aura is still one of strength.'

'Oh shit.' Kira passed the roach back. 'Auras? You're going there?'

'I think you've been stranger places.'

William regarded her with a gaze that held zero judgement, zero angst or wariness, just gentle concern. Kira turned away, fuzzy headed and now wishing her frozen moment included only her. A solo high.

'Yeah, well...'

They sat in silence. In the distance the sun pressed its way over the fields, and Kira's cute thoughts came back out to play. Fields were so damn pretty. Green had to be the prettiest colour in the world. The whole world should be green. Kermit should be king.

'Kira, can you tell me anything about the woman who attacked you in the parking lot?'

Oh yes. She could tell him that the woman's tits were natural. Two perfect, warm water balloons. She could tell him that it was possible to screw yourself into oblivion. Kira bit her bottom lip. 'I might have met her once. A long time ago.'

'Did she try to hurt you?'

'Only cause I wanted her to.' Her words dribbled out.

'Pardon?'

Kira cleared her throat, pulled herself back down off her cloud. 'No. She didn't hurt me. I don't know much about her. And she was all about the A-man. Said he was . . . impossible.'

William nodded. Slow and steady, his head a satellite tracking dish. 'Leona tells me that you believed your companion to be an AI of sorts initially,' he said. 'Do you still feel that way now?'

William's words sent a brush of something prickly up the back of her neck. She shrugged. But he was fixed on Azrael, like an art lover seeing the Mona Lisa for the first time.

'Leona talks a lot.' Kira paused, fought a pathetic fight against the words, then surrendered. 'He's not AI. I know he's not AI. I have no fucking idea what my sister has done, but I'm not sure it's anything good. I have zero clue what to do about it. This is fucked, all of this. I don't want to be here. I just want to go home.'

So it turns out the old 'weight off your shoulders' adage was not just a saying. Those cumbersome lumps left her with a thunk, her guts spilling and flopping into the air. Kira wrapped her arms around herself, hugging her ribs, ignoring the too-hard press of her metal fingers. Fully clothed but feeling naked as a stripper.

'Kira.' William didn't touch her, but his voice stilled her. 'Please know that you are safe here. Vail told me of the things that have happened. I'm sorry you're going through this. Your sister put a great burden on you, asking this of you.'

'She hasn't . . . she's not put anything . . .' The words flared and died. Dissolving into the lies they were. Blake had treated her like she was invisible for a very long time, then called her in from the cold and dumped her in a huge cesspool of shit. Even the chillax strength of the weed couldn't hold back the anger. It tied Kira's gut into knots. 'Can you see him?' She jerked her head towards Azrael. 'See what he is? Leona keeps calling him the "bright one". What does that even mean?'

There was no darkness to hide in now. Sunlight fell on them, still weak but strong enough to banish the shadows. Bradley had given up his spot on Azrael's shoulder, bored with horse worship, and lay prone on William's outstretched leg, happy as a lizard on a kaftan.

'I do see him, Kira,' William said. 'His aura, it's like trying to look into the sun. I don't know his true name, but by the Maiden's grace I believe he is an ancient thing. The Maiden is a new god, and her strength is a mere whisper of what it will become. But others came before her. Sowed the seeds for her birth. She fills a void left by them. I believe Azrael is an echo from a divine past.

I'm sorry to say that I agree with you, I do not believe your sister has done this world good. We need to know her intent.'

'Their intent.'

'I'm sorry?'

'Blake didn't just wake up and say, hey, I'm going to unleash a demon today. She's not in this alone.'

There were the ETs. But it wasn't time to go quite that far yet. And definitely not when the fence posts were swaying like palm trees.

'No, of course.' William stroked Bradley from tip of head to tip of tail, fingers tracing the bumps of orange down his sides. 'Perhaps she herself is unaware.'

Would have been nice if he'd corrected her use of the word 'demon'. 'Yeah, perhaps.'

Blake designed stuff for war. She was already dancing with the devil. A big chunk of the Facility's money came from military contracts. Okay, no nukes, but lots of creepy robot cats with no heads, and other robotic shit designed to make it easier to kill people. Safe to say, Blake wasn't a tree-hugging hippy. She was aware.

Kira couldn't forget the look on Blake's face when she'd stormed in with Azrael, and told her to take him away and not come back, no matter what she heard. The fact there had been any look at all on her sister's usually hardened face was concerning enough. Blake was Miss Stoney-face of the century, and she'd been as ruffled as shit. Kira's thoughts roller-coastered to the news about the explosion. So she was just supposed to ignore that, too? And the wings? And being wanted for murder?

She reached for the joint, and William handed it over without a pause.

'I do not expect you to agree right now,' William continued. 'But if you will permit me, I could use the combined strength of the others here to see if we can reach a little deeper into Azrael's consciousness. Maybe we can find a name. A true name.'

'He doesn't get hurt.' The directive snapped out of her. 'Don't do it, if it will hurt him.'

She bobbed along on her cloudy hash pony, watching Az play with the real ponies. Maybe she was going stark bloody bonkers, but she decided then and there, she'd kick the ass of anyone who hurt him. Demon, freak, monster, robot, whatever the fuck he was, no one got to kick Azrael's ass.

'I promise you,' William said, softly and all agreeable.

Kira nodded. If William kept his promise, then she'd tell him more. She'd tell him Azrael was not the only one.

'I want to call my sister.' The strands of grass morphed into a tiny army of cheering supporters. *Go, Kira, go.*

William settled back on his elbows, and Bradley slithered into the grass. 'Certainly. Leona told me that you do not recall the number, though.'

The green army went silent, little strands all bunched with tension. 'I'm not doing any hypnosis shit.' Her thought roller coaster headed up the steep incline. Ready for the gut-wrench dipper. 'There's a number I want to try.' Been bugging her since she'd realised it was the only number she remembered.

'All right.' William dusted off his hands as though he'd just finished gardening and dug a hand into what presumably was a pocket. Either that or he was scratching his balls. 'Then use mine.' He handed over a flip-top that was smaller than her palm and disconcertingly warm after being in its hidey-hole. The Santa smile went into overdrive. If she'd been five, she would have crawled into his lap. Hell, the way the kaftan's material draped over his package, she might do it anyway. Sex was all part of his Maiden's gig, right? And it beat the hell out of dealing with this shit.

Santa got to his feet, taking his gifts with him. 'I will leave you alone to make the call. But please, come up to the house. I'm sure you are as hungry as me right now.'

Kira stifled a puffy-cloud smile, and William continued, 'Let our chef Caleb fix you some breakfast. He makes toasted cheese sandwiches to die for.'

'Such talent.'

'He also gives incredible massages. You must try one while you're here.'

'Multi-talented.'

William adjusted the sleeves of his kaftan. 'You are all safe here, Kira. I hope you know that.'

Kira stayed as silent as her tiny green crowd. There wasn't much to say. Hard to feel safe when you didn't know what you were trying to be safe from. William whistled as he walked up the expanse of lawn towards the house. Kira and her grass army were alone. With Azrael. And Bradley. Jesus, that lizard had a hard-on for Az.

'Fuck's sake, just do it.' She flipped open the phone. The screen was cracked, but the signal was strong. Kira held her finger over the first number. Five. The grass roared, her new mates rallying her. She dialled the rest of the number. If it went to voicemail, she'd lose her shit. Simple as that. Hearing his voice, in the middle of all this, that was a deal-breaker.

The only number she remembered. Because it was a combination of birthdates. Hers, Blake's, their mum's. And Dad's.

It was the number Blake had dialled a minute before the crash. Kira had taken one hand off the wheel when the call connected, trying to swipe the phone out of her dad's hand. Taking her eyes off the road to shout at Blake that if she was cancelling on them again, she could get fucked.

Kira poked at the phone way harder than necessary. It was a fucking Hail Mary shot, but whatever was going on with Blake had propelled her into full-on dead-daddy mode; the shoes she'd put on Azrael, the place in Melgrove she'd booked as their hideout.

The call connected.

'Kira?'

'Fuck.' Kira jumped to her feet. Fence posts gyrated like belly-dancers, and her green army went ballistic.

'Kira, are you okay?'

Not ghost dad. A hush came over the crowd.

'Rossiter? What the hell? Is Blake—'

'Alive. She sent me to find you. You need to tell me where you are.'

Kira stared at the sweep of fields and unfamiliar mountains. 'I have no fucking clue.'

Eron - 25

The Bell 525 lifted off the helipad and rose over the Facility. Eron sat with his back to the cockpit in one of eight high-backed leather seats that formed a ring in the cabin's interior. Three of the other seats were occupied. Bel sat beside the window at the back of the cabin and had not spared Eron a glance or a word since they'd boarded. Indeed, longer. The heavy silence bore down on Eron, as oppressive as the presence of those in the cabin. The evacuation had been hurried, coming far sooner than intended; but the state of the level eleven chamber and the compromised cells designed to hold the Four had necessitated an early move to the external base awaiting them. Two of the Four rode with them: Agar, the gallu that had incapacitated Gren less than twenty-four hours ago; and Diresh, a gallu encapsulated in a female carapace. Both were deeply inhibited by the thick cuffs around both ankles and wrists, with another panel of Telteriun covering their eyes. The darkness appeared to subdue them naturally. Not as it had done for Azrael. The gallu had nearly torn himself apart when the lights of his cell were extinguished.

Eron traced a fingertip around the mea stone embedded in his wrist. Most of the sand-coloured stone was hidden beneath flesh that still appeared pink and raw, despite the multitude of years that had passed since the stone's interment. Not only did the site imitate a burn visually, it ached as though freshly pulled from the flames.

Slouching in his seat, Eron didn't bother to push back his silver hair as it fell across his face, grateful it blocked his view of the gallu beside him. He exhaled. 'Is this going to continue for long, Bel?' His brusque words might ignite Bel's temper, but it was preferable to sitting here in silence, head filled with the image of Agar's stare. 'This was the captain's call, not mine.'

'Your presence concerns me very much,' Bel replied after a pause. 'I'll make no secret of that.'

'You have indeed made none. Nor has Parator. At least
Cym and Seder found it within themselves to make eye contact
when the captain selected me for the Meld with Agar.' A shudder
passed through Eron as he uttered the gallu's name.

'Cym was far too gracious. He would have made a better –'

'Cym is an officer of medicine,' Eron said. 'Gren needs
him, as does Tamas. As might we all, once the hunt begins.'

Bel peered at him, the first time since they'd begun
preparations. His jet-black hair was pulled tight off his face, the
length coiled at the back of his head. The older Syranian's heavy
brow always lent a sadness to his expression, even more defined
now.

'You are a god-soldier, Eron,' Bel said. 'A warrior of Lahar.
But your discipline fails you. You made foolish mistakes, and I'm
not convinced your predilection for the humans won't inspire more
error.'

Eron fought the urge to admonish his brother. The
ceaseless doubt was growing unbearable.

'You're entitled to your concerns, of course,' he said, tone
rubbed clear of emotion. 'But you exaggerate my propensity for
error.'

'Do I, Eron?' There was weight behind the words.

Eron tried to hold Bel's gaze, but the intensity of it ruffled
him. He turned instead to the window. The great panes of glass
afforded a grand view. Below them, the Facility's main building was

61

a khaki-roofed L-shape. Dotted around it, for a radius of a couple of kilometres were warehouses and smaller buildings whose purpose Eron had never investigated. The entire complex was cradled on all sides by a low mountain range. And, invisible to the naked eye, the Lucentshield formed a barrier between the outside world and the Facility. From the air there was little to indicate the immense importance of the place. Nor the damage the Fours' arrival inflicted.

Agar's escape attempt had all but destroyed the elevator system he'd entered, and some of the ventilation shafts had suffered also. The structural integrity of the entire location was also under investigation due to the seismic activity noted with the Four's violent entrance into this world. Whether the impact of their arrival had been underestimated to begin with, or simply not considered, Eron had not yet learned.

The helicopter banked left and took them over a row of buildings he had no trouble in recognising. Kira's townhouse was the second from the left in a row of five. Beyond the accommodations, he spotted the first external hint of damage. Two air vents loosed thin grey lines of smoke into the air.

Bel's voice disturbed Eron's observations. 'A great many of them will die.'

He drew his gaze from Kira's rarely used townhouse. 'Of what exactly do you speak?'

'A great number of the humans will lose their lives in the time it takes to find Dumuzi. You understand that.'

'I'm aware that there will be loss,' Eron said. 'As there has been loss on Syrana every day since the Living Gods began their battle to ascend. The mortal are fodder. That is the way of divine war. I understand what we do here; I have never forgotten. We do this to protect Syrana.'

Bel's expression grew pained, losing its hostile edge. 'Remember more fiercely, my brother. I beg you. What we will do here cannot be done with torn loyalty.'

'An indiscretion is hardly a show of torn loyalty.'

'If it takes place only once, no, perhaps not.' Bel leaned forward in his seat, hands clasped. 'We are not gods ourselves; we make mistakes. I understand the wavering of your devotion, truth be told, I do. For so long, we waited and have done little. But it was all for this. Look at where we are.' He gestured to the silent passengers. 'It begins. I pray for you, my brother, I pray that you remember you are a god-soldier.' Unease rattled through his words.

Eron frowned. 'What is this about, Bel?'

'I observed you, Eron.' Bel sat back in his seat, letting his gaze move to the world passing beneath them.

'Observed me?' The air was uncomfortably dry. Eron cleared his throat. His eyes darted to the black carry-all shoved between the seats. It was mostly essential items, his personal effects. But one item was far more personal than the others.

'In the chamber,' Bel said.

Eron's relief was short-lived as Bel continued. 'I saw you protect the Technician. How your instinct drove you to her, the fear on your face. That was not the look of someone who understands his mistake.'

'She is integral to the—'

'She is integral to Kira,' Bel said. 'Have you forgotten how many times I've dragged you from the shrine before the captain arrived for service? I thought I saw fervour in your repentance. I believed you had taken your punishment with all seriousness and kept your distance from the girl, from her world. Yet, at the first sign of discord you sought to protect the human closest to her. I fear what else you may protect.'

'I am not privy to Kira's location, if that is what you seek.'

'I know. And that is my point. You are far too readable when it comes to her. It pains you that you don't know Kira's location. Your concern is etched in your countenance. I fear for you, Eron, and what your failure to dissolve this attachment to the human may mean for us all.'

Eron looked to where Agar sat, immovable beneath his bindings and blindfold. Blake's structural designs had gone through quite the evolution. To begin, her humanoids were all fine lines and gentle curves. Azrael's beauty showed her lightness of mind, but Agar reflected how deep her shadows had burrowed. He was her final build, and the design reeked of threat and menace.

'The girl is not an issue. Your concern is appreciated but misplaced.'

'You will need all your strength here, Eron,' Bel said. 'We may control the carapaces with the mea stones, but we must also control ourselves.'

The pilot guided them beyond the boundaries of the Facility, passing through the section where the Lucentshield would have been retracted to allow them passage. The force field embraced the entire complex and cloaked energy signatures – both preternatural and human made – from the outside world. It rendered the Syranians, and all they did there, invisible. So far as this world was concerned, Eron and his brethren did not exist.

But that would change now.

For the remainder of the two-hour journey, Eron kept his eyes closed, pretending to doze. He opened them only when the downward tilt of the aircraft announced their arrival in the city. The cycle of Dumuzi's resurrections shifted in a recurring pattern all over this world. Occurring on one continent after another in a never-ending cycle. His lifespan was always the same, thirty-five years, the demigod never growing older beyond the age when Inanna had betrayed him. But his precise location within that pattern was not information even Lahar and Ereshkigal could draw upon. The gods had taken an educated guess. No one, not even Tamas, knew exactly how the goddess had decided on the required continent, nor indeed how she'd chosen the geographic triangulation they should commence their search in. It was an enormous area of land, roughly triangular, encompassing three human cities— New Weston in the north, Telbourne in the south west, and Valens to the south east, where Seder and Parator had been assigned with the two other gallu.

The Four had been divided, in order to conquer.

Ground zero for Eron and Bel was here, in New Weston, the largest of the three. A metropolitan home to nearly eight million humans. The pilot guided the helicopter's considerable bulk down onto the roof of one of the tallest skyscrapers in view. Eron had not frequented this city before. On the trio of outings he'd had with Kira, she'd kept him within a hundred-kilometre radius of the base, amongst small towns, at best a few hundred thousand in the populace.

Now, eight million people. And they sought only one soul amongst them.

In their favour was the fact that Dumuzi's path was set and could not be diverted from for his life cycle. He could not leave the coordinates he'd been birthed into. The randomness of divine rules rendered the demigod a fish that could not leave its tank.

Eron stepped from the aircraft, and a hot blast of humid air encased him, playing havoc with the strands of his hair. He left Bel in his wake, not in the mood for any more sanctimonious discussion. Several armed personnel, three women and a man, strode past him with a cursory nod. They pushed twin carts with rounded containment capsules. Each gallu would be placed and restrained in these before being moved from the craft. Eron brushed at the front of his fitted jacket, though it needed no adjustment. He needed something to do with his hands, the arrival here having set his pulses into hurried rhythms. The goddess had played her hand as far as was possible. What came next depended on the Four. And the god-soldiers who held them in check.

Eron strode towards the glass doors on the left-hand side of the rooftop. The automatic panels might have made a sound as they slid back to accommodate him, but the thunderous noise from the helicopter dwarfed it. He stepped into the welcome embrace of air-conditioning and a sparsely furnished foyer, pausing to tidy the wind-blown mess of his hair.

'This way.' Bel overtook him and headed through a wooden door the colour of liquorice, its golden handle glinting. The room they stepped into could never be described as sparse. It was a lounging room of sorts, judging by the surplus of opulent couches, curved burgundy monstrosities laden with embroidered cushions and trimmed with the same shade of gold as the door handle. Floor-to-ceiling glass offered an uninterrupted view of the city. Eron stopped beneath a chandelier, its twinkling artificial light dancing around him. After years mostly confined underground, he couldn't decide if the room's sense of space moved him or disquieted him. A little of both, he suspected.

The late afternoon sun hid behind a neighbouring building, and elongated shadows stretched across city streets far below.

'Apologies for the unpreparedness.' A feminine voice filled the room. 'Tamas didn't expect the adjustment period would take place outside the Facility so it has been quite the task to ready for your arrival.' A woman entered the room; Eron recognised her but failed to recall a name. Her skin was the colour of evening, her head crowned with an explosion of tight brown curls. A tailored houndstooth suit and high-necked cream blouse appeared sewn onto her curves. 'Hello, gentlemen. It has been quite some time since I've been in your company, it is good to see you again. My name is Clara. Mr Cressly asked me to attend to your needs while you are here.'

Now Eron recalled. The woman had been less well groomed when she'd worked as liaison between the Facility and those who had hired the elite super-squad Tamas could provide. Clara had been present on both the contracts Eron had been involved in, journeying with the Syranians to a place where rainforest soaked the landscape and threatened to swallow them all whole. Each time, a delivery of some kind had taken place, the Syranians tasked with moving a cargo through unstable territory. These contracts, undoubtedly beyond legal boundaries, had been intended to alleviate boredom and exercise the Syranians' military muscles. Eron would readily have remained underground if it meant never gracing those rain-drenched forests again.

'We require refreshments and then to be taken to the containment area. Preparations must begin immediately,' Bel said.

'Of course, the meals are ready for you. This way please, gentlemen.'

Everything about her spoke of attention to detail, from her polished fingernails to her carefully applied make-up. Eron committed her subtle eyeshadow to memory, a glorious conglomerate of greens. Cosmetics fascinated him, though he'd learned quickly his classification as a male on this planet vetoed his involvement publicly with the application. The brown eyes beneath the appealing eyeshadow had barely left Bel since they'd arrived. Clara stared at him so intently Eron wondered if Bel had forgotten to put his contacts in. It wasn't the case; Bel's irises were a soft shade of blue, his preferred colour.

She led them into a dining room, where a marble table capable of seating eight was set for just two. Clara pulled out a seat and gestured to it. 'Eron, would you like to sit here?'

He nodded. Clara's gaze lingered a fraction too long as he took his seat, and there seemed no evident reason for her hand to brush his shoulder.

'Please take the opportunity to relax.' If she noted Bel's frown, she ignored it. 'There will be little respite, I'm afraid. Mr Cressly would like to attempt to take the assets out tomorrow. It is a public holiday here, a day to honour a historical figure whose name will mean little to you. In a serendipitous twist, there has recently been catastrophic weather in some rather poor parts of the world. So the lovely citizens here have organised what they call a fundraiser. A huge parade, a dance music event, everyone out celebrating their ability to assist their fellow man.' Clara paused her rather dry telling and darted her tongue across her blood-red lips. 'It will run all day and into the evening. They are expecting a substantial crowd as the weather will be perfect, hence our intention to utilise the event. It will be a colourful affair, a place where everyone' – her gaze darted between each of them – 'will fit in without any concern. They are expecting tens of thousands of people. We weren't prepared to begin this early, but as you are here, Mr Cressly deemed it fortuitous.'

Tens of thousands of people. Eron focused on the waiter serving his meal, refusing to raise his head and meet the scrutiny he knew Bel levelled at him.

The waiter, dressed in immaculately pressed beige linen, placed a rectangular plate in front of him. Dabs of coloured sauce ringed a singular piece of steak and curls of something that might have been orange potato. Eating would be difficult; the events of the past twenty-four hours had rid him of any appetite.

'Is Tamas's recovery progressing well?' Eron toyed with the meat. Dead animal, Kira would remind him. Yet again his thoughts drifted to where she might be. How she was faring. Eron stabbed the knife point deep into the carcass.

'Very well,' Clara said. 'The surgery was successful, the bone reset. He is awake and mobile. I'm due to speak with him momentarily, as a matter of fact.'

'And Gren?' Bel spoke through a mouthful. 'Any new estimates?'

'Full recovery will be complete within forty-eight hours. I'll be back to escort you to the containment area but must leave you now. Please, excuse me, gentleman. And let me know if you require anything else at all.'

Brandis mer. Did the woman need to punctuate her words with such a pointed stare? Eron shifted in his chair, thrusting a forkful of the orange curls into his mouth. There had been several humans like this, male and female, since word of his indiscretion with Kira had spread in the Facility. The sexual appetites of humans were indeed complex. And far more voracious than his own. In that, he and Kira could not have been more opposite. It was company he'd sought, not just the touch of flesh.

Attachment.

Clara left them, and only the clatter of cutlery disturbed the silence. Eron managed to empty his plate and nodded when the waiter asked if he would like another serving. Perhaps another chunk of dead animal would fill the hollow that had sat at his core since the Final Meld. He could not chance asking Bel if he experienced the same empty sensation. An answer in the negative would only further fuel his brother's doubts.

Bel threw his cutlery onto an empty plate, the sharp sound startling Eron from his thoughts. 'You did not appear pleased with Gren's recovery time.' He sat back in his chair. 'Too soon, or not soon enough?'

Eron pushed his plate away and stood up. 'Do not taunt me, Bel. I am tired of it.'

He gestured to the waiter and asked to be taken to his quarters. The copious servings of food had not had their desired effect, the hollow still evident deep within.

'You did not answer my question, Eron.'

Nor did he intend to. For he had no certain answer to give.

Tamas - 26

The shadows crept across the low mountains, fingers spreading across the desert, snaking their way through the tall reeds of the water garden beyond Tamas's window. He lay propped up in his bed. His head was swathed in bandages, and twin tubes of plastic fed oxygen into his nostrils. A faint tang of chemicals hung in the air, and the monotonous pulse of the monitoring equipment tracked his vitals. The woozy clutches of anaesthetic were now completely erased, no longer hiding the ache throughout his body.

It grew stronger with each hour of recovery. Bone deep, something physical resting within his marrow.

Tamas couldn't handle the itch beneath his skin any longer and raked his fingernails the length of his arms. He'd heard of drug addicts ripping at their skin, drawing blood, to try to get at the bugs they were so certain were beneath the layers, but he'd never expected he'd learn exactly what that felt like. Ereshkigal had not returned him from the dreamscape alone. And her 'gift' of the utukku was not one he would have chosen for himself. Tamas paused in his attempts to ease the itch, catching voices in the hall beyond his room. They passed by, and he returned to scratching, edging his finger under the cast on his left arm.

The aftermath of the Final Meld was a semiconscious blur, but clearly he'd broken his wrist. He recognised the intricate design of the cast encasing his injury. Blake had based the structure on sea-fan coral, a deceptively delicate pattern created via a 3D printer; much stronger than its plaster predecessor and more conducive to healing. Fine wiring embedded in the material enabled ultrasound therapy to heal breaks faster. He ran his free hand over the smooth material: a mix of nylon, carbon fibre, and titanium. This cast was where it had all begun, Blake's first construct after she'd started work at the Facility. The patent still brought in a nice royalty.

The swell of grief came out of nowhere. That time, and that relationship they'd had, was long gone. Tamas swallowed hard. Fixing his thoughts on the truth of things. The reason he lay here, fighting the urge to take a knife to his skin and dig out the utukku beneath it, was because of her. Blake's betrayal. Tamas pressed his head against the pillow, clutching at the sheets. She'd asked him before the Final Meld, *What have we done?*

He'd done what he'd been told. Done what he'd been born to do. Follow the rules. Bow to the divine. Grief morphed to anger. Who the hell did Blake think she was? He'd given her the technological nirvana she was so obsessed with, and it still wasn't enough. She'd messed with things, and Tamas suffered for it. He slammed his hand down on the call button at his bedside, and the door slid open almost immediately. The nurse who'd been there when he'd first awoken raced into the room. A mousy-haired man, no older than Tamas himself.

'Mr Cressly? Is everything all right?'

Tamas's simmering anger gave him the strength to glare at the man.

'I'm fine. Is Ms Beckworth here yet?'

He'd summoned her fifteen minutes ago. Blake's work was done. Reuben had advised Tamas that the Four had been transported to the external bases about half an hour ago. On top of everything else, Tamas hadn't even had a chance to see them in the flesh. Forced to view them on a tablet screen from his bed.

'About five minutes away, sir. She's in the elevator —'

'I didn't ask for details. Nari was to be sent to me some time ago too. Where is she?' His heart thudded with the force of his words, but his skin was cool. No blush. Just the nagging itch. So busy marvelling at himself, Tamas was slow to notice the nurse's pained expression. 'Is there a problem?'

The nurse glanced towards the door.

'Answer me.' The nurse jumped, the snap of Tamas's voice shocking them both.

'Sir, yes. I'm so sorry . . .'

The door to the room slid open, and Blake was ushered in by two guards. Reuben followed in behind them. The nurse's relief was a visible thing, shoulders dropping and a sigh quickly stifled.

'Get out.'

The nurse didn't need to be told twice, hurrying from the room. Blake hugged herself, biting on her bottom lip. Her hair was loose, knots evident in the strands. The left side of her face had a coin-sized circle of purplish bruising. She didn't ask how he was doing. Nor did she glance his way.

Reuben gestured for the guards to leave, which they did almost as quickly as the nurse. Tamas noted the state of Blake's clothes. The same clothes she'd been wearing at the Final Meld. Black pants patched with paler blotches of dust and dirt, a tear at the right thigh. His eyes fell on the dark brown stains marking the white linen of her shirt at her waistline. Little doubt it was blood.

He returned his attention to Reuben. 'Where is Nari?'

But the guard didn't need to answer. The way he avoided eye contact said it all. Tamas pulled the sheet in tighter around his chest.

'Why did you not tell me earlier?' The words bubbled low and sharp, and the hairs on Tamas's arms rose.

Reuben, a hulking, formidable man, seemed to shrink in on himself. 'It did not seem to be the time, you were –'

Tamas picked up a glass of water from his bedside and hurled it at his guard. 'Get out, get out of here.'

The itch turned to bubbling heat. The utukku strained beneath his flesh, goosebumps so rounded they tried to burst from his skin entirely.

'Sir –'

Tamas grabbed the first thing at hand. The remote for the TV. It flew from his hand, and something ripped from his fingertips. A scream catapulted from deep in Tamas's chest. Reuben lifted off his feet, his body hurtling across the room, smashing into the concrete wall, and thumping onto the floor. The guard groaned, crouching on all fours. He raised his head. Tiny specks of red coated his face, like a sudden and severe case of the measles. The door flew open, and the two guards who'd brought in Blake rushed into the room, stopping dead when they saw Reuben on his knees. Tamas's own scream echoed in his ears. His hand was still outstretched in front of him, and his chest was heaving. Tiny specks lifted in a hazy miniature cloud away from Reuben and drifted across the space, finding their way to Tamas's outstretched fingers. Tamas sucked in his breath. The minute particles burrowed into the torn skin at his fingertips. It stung like salt on an open cut, but Tamas didn't flinch. He curled his fingers into his palm, blood smearing his skin – and elation lifting the edges of his mouth. Power. Real power.

One of his puppet strings had been cut.

He relished the sensation a moment longer, then looked up. Blake's mouth hung open, and her skin, already so insipidly pale after so many hours underground, had reached an ashen shade. Her fingers rested on her chin, as though the shock had stopped them from reaching her mouth to cover a gasp. She wasn't quite as unscathed as he'd first believed. One hand was heavily bandaged. But it wasn't just physical wounds. It was something more drilled down; it sucked at her cheeks and dampened the light in her eyes. He'd not noticed when she got so skinny.

'Tamas . . .' Whatever she thought to say made it no further, fading into oblivion.

Her hesitation buoyed him. For once, he was not the speechless one. His nerves buzzed with the thrill of it.

'You asked me what we have done. Blake, we've walked with the gods.' Tamas's smile reawakened, splitting cracked lips. 'I wanted to share that to you. I gave you that gift. But it wasn't enough. You shouldn't have interfered. Azrael was never yours to take. Did you really think you could just do what you wanted?'

Reuben used the wall to help himself to his feet, eyes fixed on Tamas, bracing as if he expected another blow. 'And you, Reuben, should not take it on yourself to determine what I can and can't hear.'

Reuben and Blake were amongst a handful of people in this world he'd ever held some semblance of feeling for. And they'd both shafted him.

'Yes, sir.' Reuben nodded, his skin was blistered with red welts. And for the first time, he sounded as he had when he'd served Tamas's mother. Subservient. Under control.

Tamas lifted the covers and swung his legs over the side of the bed. He ripped the IV drip from his arm. The itch resettled beneath his skin, but not half as irritating as before. As though the entities he carried weren't so keen to leave him anymore.

'Blake, come here.' He adjusted his bedclothes, white cotton with blue piping on the edges. Egyptian cotton. Priced to feed a family of four for a week. He'd worn nothing less for a good ten years.

Blake wrestled against the guards as they dragged her to his bedside. 'I've already told you what I know, Tamas. You made sure of that, remember?'

Tamas's broad smile returned, and a bubble of laughter rose in his chest. 'Yeah, that stung a little, huh?' The trace of guilt that had come at the time he'd used the serum on her was nowhere to be found now. He took her face in his bloodied hands. Not even a hint of pain within his fractured wrist. She trembled. 'And I suspect this will hurt just the same. If not more.'

He barely recognised his own voice. Deeper, rumbling. Not a tremor. He drew Blake closer, and the utukku went into overdrive. The itch morphed into a vibration that tried to shake a rib loose. And Tamas didn't give a damn. Blake kicked out at him. She missed and her shin smacked against the bedframe. She gripped hold of his wrists, her fingers slipping over the smooth surface of the cast. Her own creation hindering her.

'What is happening to you, Tamas?' she hissed.

'You should be worried about what is happening to you, Blake.'

He brought his mouth near hers, the closest he'd been to those lips in at least ten years. To any lips, for that matter. Tamas had no intention of getting any closer, but the sheer horror on her face hardened his resolve beyond any doubt. Stupid bitch. As if he wanted her. Or anything so trivial, anymore. The utukku rose up beneath his skin. His hands were swollen, bulging with the power beneath them, his body heated as though inflammation sat at every joint.

'This isn't you, Tamas.' Blake tilted her head away from him.

'But I want it to be.' Pressure behind his eyes seemed intent on shoving them from their sockets. If this was but a taste of what was to come, he wanted every last damn drop. 'Why the sudden conscience, Blake? We've been feeding the war machine for years. And we did an amazing fucking job.'

Blake relaxed in his grip, let her hands drop to her sides. 'We didn't start those wars, and we knew all about the ones we were involved in.' She fixed amber eyes on his. 'I took Azrael because I was pissed he was going to be thrown away, my work treated like it was a pile of trashable shit. But I thought I was stealing some goddamn AI, a hunter like you said. I thought I knew what I was building. What the hell happened to Perry? And those women at the hotel? I know you haven't found Kira, or Azrael. You're a lying piece of shit, and a bad one. But something is tracking them. Killing people. What happens when the rest of the carapaces are out there? Tell me what I've created, tell me what war we've just started.'

Her voice bounced around his skull, too high and uncomfortable. Tamas tightened his grip, and her lips pursed. 'Don't flatter yourself. You hardly fired the first shot. I offered you a chance to be a player, and you took it – then threw it in my face. Now, you've made my life more complicated than it needs to be, and I don't like complicated. So let's fix that. You have one final thing I need, then I'll let the goddess tell you herself how much she disapproves of what you did. You're going to suffer, Blake. And just remember, you brought it all on yourself.'

Tamas dug his fingernails into her skin, sinking them down like hooks. Letting his fish wriggle beneath them. The hatred flowed. All he had to do was recall Blake's face in the chamber before he'd stepped into the Waters. The disdain. Disgust. He added Eron's face to the memory. The Syranian needed only to have given him the barest glance. A simple look to acknowledge Tamas's existence, but he had failed to do even that. Doing as they all did. Even his own mother. Treating Tamas as if he were the piece of trashable shit Blake spoke about.

Big mistake.

The memories were tinder, and the uttuku were sparks. They raced through his pores, cutting their way to his hands. Blake's eyes widened, a choked sound coming from her open mouth. She tried to shake her head, but he held fast. Digging his grip harder. Tamas gritted his teeth against the rush of tiny pellets tearing their way through his palms. Bittersweet agony. Sharp as razors, the grains of Ereshkigal's sand pummelled into Blake's cheeks.

Blood, warm and bright, seeped from Tamas's hands. His and Blake's, blending together as the utukku sank into her cells.

No. He hadn't found Kira. But the utukku would. They were blooded hounds now. Fat on the genetic code that would lead them to Kira. Blake's memories had been a dead end, but her DNA was not. And whatever warped luck had seen Kira able to keep Enkidu hidden from them would run out now.

Tamas let his head drop back, punch-drunk on the frenzy beneath his skin. He released Blake, and she dropped to the floor, lifting shaking hands to her bleeding face. But remaining infuriatingly silent.

'Take her to the Orientation Room. I'll join you shortly.'

The two guards jogged to Blake's side, one of them skidding on a smear of blood on the floor. She warded them back with crimson palms. 'Fuck off. I can walk.'

Blake used the bed to stagger to her feet, leaving a crimson palm print on the white sheet. She stepped back. Swaying but remaining upright. It surprised and irritated Tamas. He wasn't so certain he could keep his own footing if he got off the bed. 'Reuben —'

'Yes, sir.' The man who had been at his side since the day Tamas's mother died showed no visible discomfort about what he'd just witnessed. Good thing, considering what Tamas would ask of him next. The other two guards escorted Blake towards the door.

'Miss Beckworth has kindly given us what we need.' Tamas's eyes traced Blake's path. Only the tiniest waver betrayed her unsteadiness. 'You're going to assemble a team, four should do it. Along with some grimalkin. You will bring in the Lesser and the stolen property.'

'Yes, sir,' Reuben said. 'Where would you have me go?'

'Beleiro. There is already a small team on the ground there after the murders were reported.' Looking for a preternatural needle in a haystack, an indication of what direction Kira had fled in. 'But now we have the tools which will enable us to see the situation in a very different light. Come here, Reuben. I will need you to take those tools with you.'

The guard's stony expression didn't shift, but his eyes did dart, ever so briefly, to the splotch of blood on the floor.

Tamas offered the guard a gentle smile. 'I will do what I can to make this as comfortable as possible. We'll be sharing the burden.'

Reuben nodded and knelt beside the bed, his greater height placing his head in the perfect position for Tamas to touch his bloodied hands to his cheeks.

'Ready yourself,' Tamas whispered.

Reuben closed his eyes, and the uttuku bloodhounds tore their way into the body of the last remaining human on Earth Tamas trusted.

Blake - 27

Blake stared at her reflection in the closed elevator doors, barely recognising the smudged, damaged mess gazing back at her. The guards flanking her—the same women who'd accompanied her to the medical ward—waited restlessly. The slighter of the two muscular escorts tapped an unsettled tune against her weapon. Blood seeped from the shallow markings on Blake's face. Whatever Tamas had just done, it was as though it had torn open each and every pore and doused it with salt. But the pain went deeper than that. Something far more terrible than broken skin.

Tamas told her she was to suffer. And should remember she'd brought it all on herself. Certain aspects of that statement were undeniably true. A bloody drop fell away from Blake's chin and hit the corridor tiles, leaving an intricate splash of crimson on the white surface. The elevator doors opened, and the musical guard poked her in the back with a semi-automatic. Blake's skin flared with pain, every nerve ending on edge.

'Don't touch me,' she said.

The guard mumbled an apology, but her pinch-faced companion glared at her. 'Get in, Blake. Let's not make this difficult.'

Certainly, no one wanted difficult. Blake stepped into the elevator, leaving a short trail of crimson in her wake. The front of her cotton blouse was now home to several more stains. The peach fabric darkened pink with fresh blood, and smudges of brown where older bloodstains had dried. At least her palm was still numb after the sutures, one part of her that did not hurt. Blake toyed with the bandage wrapped around the injury, considering her options.

They were severely limited. And the plan forming in her exhausted mind bordered on ludicrous. But the magnitude of what was occurring had widened far beyond acceptable boundaries, at a speed that had caught her off guard. And she had put Kira right in the middle of it all. Blake curled her fingers into her bandages. When Tamas had touched her, there was undeniable pain, but the pain was the least of it. What moved within him—what moved *into* her— had darkened everything. And it was not some truth serum that played with her synapses, or toxic water that broke down her cells. Chemicals and disease were quantifiable. Ultimately understandable. That was what she had sought here. Knowability.

To understand the why. Of everything.

But when Tamas touched her – hurt her – the darkness that had come had no name. No label to apply. No code to decipher. As unknowable as death.

And it frightened her more than anything she had ever seen in the Facility.

The metal box lowered her down into a private hell; a place comprehension could not breach.

Level two.

Level three.

Blake had taken too long to come up for air. She hadn't wanted to take a breath from what she was discovering at the Facility. Tamas worshipped his gods, and Blake had fawned over her own – physics, math, engineering – ignoring the cost. But now, finally, the oxygen had been forced into her lungs. And she found herself here. Slowly dying. And a walking, talking line straight out of the book her father had gifted her, the book that had gathered dust since the day he'd handed it to her.

'I am become death, destroyer of worlds.'

Level four.

Blake hadn't started the wars fought on Earth, the ones the Facility built its robots and drones for, nor had she fired the first shot in whatever battle the aliens waged for their gods. But here she was anyway. As much a part of the consequences as Tamas or the captain, or Oppenheimer.

And her ludicrous plan was all she had. All she could offer as compensation. Blake dug her fingers deep into the wound and let the agony propel a gut-wrenching scream from her. She fell to her knees. The guards, predictably, leaned in towards her. Blake sucked in a breath and thrust her elbow into the face of the shorter woman, the musician, landing a perfectly placed hit against her beaked nose.

'Fuck.' The woman grunted and reeled backwards, her gun clattering to the floor. Blake heaved herself upright. Surprise was key, Rossiter's teachings. Don't hesitate. Blake threw her body weight against the other woman. The guard was considerably bigger, but momentum was everything. And it was in Blake's favour. They crashed against the back wall of the elevator. Blake ran her hands over the guard's hip holster. Straight to the location Rossiter had drilled into her. Her fingers found the Taser.

'Blake, stop.' The guard sounded almost bemused, as though Blake was little more than a puppy trying to attack its own shadow. 'Just calm down—'

A shock of volts ripped through the guard's body. She jerked and flopped and crashed to the ground. Blake spun around and found herself face-to-face with the other woman, blood streaming from her nose, eyes watering. No bemusement there. The nozzle of her gun raised. Blake thrust the Taser into her belly. The woman's knees buckled and her eyes rolled back in her head. She dropped to the floor.

Entire body shaking, Blake leapt over the woman. The elevator had just passed level five.

'Damn it.' She pressed level six. Over and over and over. She darted a glance back. The larger woman was moving, reaching gingerly for her comms device, a silver triangle attached behind her ear. Blake's reaction was knee-jerk. She kicked out, her booted toe finding the woman's temple. The guard's head snapped back with a crack, and she collapsed, her head tilted at an odd angle against the wall of the elevator. Eyes closed.

'Oh shit.' Blake could barely hold her finger steady enough to press the elevator button. Rossiter may have prepared her to defend herself, but he couldn't have prepared her for the debilitating effects of adrenaline. Her heart rate soared, and sweat coated her face, diluting the blood and sending pale rivulets down her neck. Her knees barely held her weight.

The elevator slowed to a stop and the doors parted. Staying inside the confined space with the disabled guards, waiting for doors to slowly draw closed and haul back up a floor, took a resolve she didn't have. Blake raced out into the empty corridor, one hand tracing the wall to keep her steady. She struggled to catch her breath, throat parched. The window of opportunity would be impossibly small, but it was there.

She flung open the door to a stairwell. The advantage of living your life at work was that you knew your workplace intimately. Blake grunted, forcing one leg in front of the other. One step after another. And there were multitudes of them. At this rate Tamas would be advised of her hit-and-run before she reached level five, let alone the Research and Development lab there.

Muscles burning and heart rate at an all-time high, Blake staggered out of the stairwell and into the long corridor of level five, painted a white that always reminded her of Mediterranean villas. Blake shot glances left and right. Empty. The destruction on level eleven had some advantages. Nonessential personnel had been evacuated while the damage was being assessed. And the deserted hallway suggested that those developing high-security military assets had been included in that evacuation.

The corridor was lined with rooms, some barely big enough to accommodate two people, but all of them constructed with explosion-resistant concrete and a unique bomb-proof wallpaper that the Facility's research team had developed. One or two of the rooms were grand enough to have housed all of the carapaces if necessary. The entire level enjoyed the same level of high security and restricted access as the level eleven. The perfect place to hide a stolen item.

'Please be here,' she whispered. Her boots were disconcertingly loud against the concrete floor. Dotted along the roof of the curved corridor, black cameras eyed every step of her journey. She kept her gaze on the floor, hoping to assume some anonymity. Knowing full well it was a ridiculous notion. Everyone here knew Blake Beckworth. But she pinned her hopes on the idea that Tamas hadn't had time to send out a memo to notify them she was now persona non grata.

The room she searched for drew up on her right. Blake raised her hand to the keypad. Tamas might not have sent out a memo, but he could have had her security clearance cancelled. The door slid open, and Blake let out a relieved sigh, dashing into the room. She was so close. A few metres more and she'd have what she needed.

Moving to the row of reinforced steel drawers that took up the entire length of the back wall, she crouched down. And hesitated. Cameras did more than just reveal her location. They tracked her movements. She'd need to make it look as though she were here for something other than what rested in the third drawer down. Blake got back to her feet, using the bench to steady herself. Now that she'd stopped for a moment, her limbs grew even more jellylike. She took a deep breath, and the room tilted. A laptop sat cradled at the end of a manoeuvrable arm attached to the top of the cabinet. Blake tugged it towards her, extending the arm and positioning it to block the single camera that watched her. Hiding her hand as she lowered it, she swiped her security pass over the detection panel and opened the drawer.

'Shit,' Blake hissed between clenched teeth.

Wrong drawer. This one was home to a JHex: a shoebox-sized, passively stable six-legged robot. The design was still in early production stages and twenty times the size of the device she searched for. Blake tried again, on the drawer below, while keeping her free hand on the keyboard and attempting to make it appear that she was actually using it. Anyone astute enough might notice that not only did using a bandaged hand make typing a nearly impossible task but also that right-handed Blake Beckworth was using her left hand.

This time when the drawer eased open, she allowed herself a breath. Embedded at the back of the drawer was the lock-box she sought. A keypad put a password between the contents of the box and any curious technician. What lay inside was for this Technician only. Blake keyed in the complex passcode, the length of which tested her overburdened faculties, and the lockbox opened. Two beads of smooth amethyst-coloured crystal sat atop black velvet. As though they were jewels on display in a store – and not lethal Syranian explosives. Blake lifted them from their bed.

Starpoints. At least, that's what Kira decided to call them. She had stolen this pair from Eron, deciding they were too beautiful to be stuffed inside a pouch at his waist. It was before Blake learned that her sister and the Syrana were sharing more than conversations. She'd found Kira rolling them across the kitchen table one evening, slurring her explanation about how she'd come to have them between sips of red wine. Smile as wide as her flushed cheeks would allow. Blake had snatched them from her, ignoring her suggestion that it would be 'cool' to have a secret between sisters. Blake rubbed the smooth surface of one of the stones. She'd told Kira she was being a fool—both for her attentions towards Eron, and for meddling in things she didn't understand— and declared she would return the stones to Captain Nex immediately.

Blake'd done no such thing. For no reason she could determine. Work on the carapaces hadn't begun. But Blake's obsession with the Syrana and their technology had. She'd wheedled what information she could about the stones from Cym. According to the medic-soldier, they were mini-bombs. Devastatingly powerful. Activated by synchronised impact; crushed underfoot or in the titanic grip of a being as strong as the Syrana godsoldiers. Each of the aliens carried a pair. Several pairs. And it was at that point in the conversation Blake had decided she would not be returning the Starpoints to Captain Nex. Believing Eron would hesitate to notify his leader of their loss considering the circumstances in which he'd misplaced them, Blake could retain them unnoticed. A souvenir of sorts. She'd been proven right. And the stones had been her 'cool' secret for the years since.

One that now fortified her.

If Tamas was going to make her kneel to his mistress, Blake would not do it unarmed. Though the Four might be already out in the world, she could still destroy the place that had birthed them.

The door to the room opened, and the Starpoints almost slipped from her grasp. Blake shoved the drawer closed with her knee and turned to meet the intruder.

'Weylen.' Her voice jumped with relief. 'What are you –'

'Blake, they're looking for you –'

'I know.' And she would let them find her. Tamas wanted her in the heart. The shrine. Perfect location for a detonation.

'Ketch gave me the heads-up about what you did in the elevator. What the hell, Blake? We've given you as much time as we can, but the guys in surveillance can't stall any longer. What are you doing down here?' Weylen's black curls were a knotted mess. A bruise marked her chin, and scratches flecked her neck, but her concern was elsewhere. 'Blake, you're hurt.'

'I just need a few more minutes.' Though Blake didn't understand Weylen's attraction to the churlish head of surveillance, Ketch, the long-running affair had its advantages. 'Stand in front of me. Block the camera.'

'What?'

'Do it, Weylen.'

Her assistant moved into position, and Blake tugged the bandages from around her hand. The stitch-up was neat and tidy. The scarring would have been minimal. Pity it would not remain so. Blake scanned the bench top. Empty. Nothing sharp to aid her. But hanging around Weylen's neck, her titanium ID card.

'Give me your ID.'

Weylen frowned. 'What—'

Blake snatched it from her neck, the anti-choking mechanism releasing it. Blake pressed the card's sharp corner edge into the stitches.

'Jesus, Blake, no.'

Weylen moved to stop her, but Blake elbowed her out of the way. Lips pressed tight, cheeks bulging with a stifled cry, Blake sliced open the stitches, and shoved the Starpoints into the deep gash. She staggered against the desk, blood rushing in her ears and spilling from her palm.

Weylen grasped her, uttering a short cry. 'What are you doing? Please, tell me what's going on.'

Rewrapping the bandages tightly around the bleeding, Blake kept her head lowered. 'Tell them I was trying to log in to security to try to find Kira. I'm going to hit you now, you're going to go down. And I'm sorry.'

Weylen opened her mouth, but Blake left no opportunity for questions. She grabbed the laptop and swung it at her assistant.

The blow was nowhere near what was required to incapacitate her, but Weylen did as she was told. Crying out, staggering back.

It was time for Blake to move. But her muscles were protesting her dramatic moves in the elevator. After only ever play-acting with Rossiter, the effect of doing it for real had left her weakened. She pushed herself into a run, leaving the room and moving into the corridor. Any direction. It didn't matter. She chose right. And kept on running. This section of the corridor was lit by emergency lighting only. The scent of something metallic hung on the air. A faint hint of smoke. She sent out a silent prayer to no god in particular that Tamas's search party would locate her sooner rather than later. Her chest ached with each breath, and at any moment her knees were going to give out. The throb in her hand rose to an uncomfortable level and she fought not to think about what she'd just done.

'Blake, stop. Stop right there.' The voice boomed from deeper down the corridor. A trio of guards emerged out of the darkness with weapons raised. All faces she recognised, no names she remembered. People following orders.

Blake raised her hands, sinking to her knees. The insanity of her plan bloomed in the dullness. Stark and bright. Even after the semi-evacuation, the Facility was crammed with people just like this. And the Starpoints would obliterate every one of them.

Blake pressed her hand to her thigh until the pain blotted her vision. Whispers filled her skull, the same incessant voices that had plagued her from the moment the Waters took hold in her blood. All her choices seemed to lead her right back here. To this place.

You are become death. Destroy…this world.

Kira - 28

William hadn't exaggerated. The chef guy Caleb did indeed make cheese sandwiches worth jumping off a cliff for. Kira bit into her third one, sighing into the gooey heaven. The sandwiches were a surprisingly good distraction. As was the chef. Except for the fact that he'd whooped her ass about five times in rummy, he was okay company. The dude had more hair than a Yeti – beard, head, chest, and arms – but she wasn't holding that against him. In fact, as the day dragged on and he kept her amused, she'd become more and more intrigued with finding out exactly how much hair covered the rest of his body. He was probably touching forty, had a slight pot belly and old-man's sandals, but Kira had never been accused of being fussy. Wiping her chin, Kira glanced up at the kitchen clock. Fuck, was she in a bloody time warp? How could it be only four in the afternoon?

'It is a minute later than the last time you looked.' Caleb's blue eyes sparkled – actually sparkled – under the kitchen's unforgiving fluorescent lights. 'Your friend is not expected until tomorrow morning, no?'

Nope. It would take Rossiter and his secrets a good twenty-four hours to reach her. Well, the town of Jackson a few kilometres away. William wasn't giving away exact coordinates, and Rossiter didn't want them. Being all super spy about it, taking his time to make sure he wasn't being followed. Aside from telling her Blake wasn't dead, Rossiter had said jack shit in their phone call, keen to get the hell off the line in case anyone traced the call.

The call from her dead dad's cell phone.

Nice, Blake. Not at all fucked up. Kira tugged at the oversized shirt she'd changed into: baby pink with a faded picture of kittens in a handbasket.

'Tomorrow morning is a fucking lifetime away.' Kira slapped her cards on the bench.

'But he will come.'

Would you like to, caveman? The proposition dangled on the tip of her tongue. She hopped off the stool and bent over, touching her toes. Trying to get some blood to her head. To think clearly.

'Yeah,' she said. 'He will. He jumps when B says jump.'

Caleb rifled his way through one of the cupboards.

'Would you like to help me prepare the evening meal?' he said. 'That might distract you.'

Kira wrapped her arms around the backs of her legs, pressing her boobs tight against her thighs. Culinary delights were not entirely what she had in mind, but hey, whatever. 'Sure.'

She stood up, face hot with blood and head spinning at the sudden uprightedness. Caleb watched her, holding a small pestle and mortar, a coy smile on his face. *Oh hello, sailor. Where did those dimples come from?*

'Want me to pestle something?' She held out her flesh hand, and he laughed while placing the marble pestle on her palm, but not letting it go.

'Yes. That would be very nice of you.'

Eyes like Antarctic ice. Her smile dropped a fraction. The colour reminded her of Eron's. The barest shadow of colour beneath the white of his eyes. *Hell, no. Get over that shit, right now.* She pulled her hand away, wrapping her fingers around the pestle and slipping them ever so slightly up and down the length of the marble. Pretty basic stuff. And basic stuff worked. Caleb smiled, and blushed. Cute. He wasn't a devourer then. Desperate as her to eat someone alive in a mess of sex. No worries. Sometimes being slammed against a wall was all that would do, but today, giggles and fumbling would do just nicely.

'Kira.'

They both jumped at the voice. Kira spun round. The freckle-faced auburn-haired chick who'd barely said two words since they'd arrived stood in the doorway. Greta, her name was. Friendly, her manner wasn't. For a supposed coven, this one was sure down on numbers. It was a party of three. Just Caleb, William, and Greta, who looked about early twenties, probably no older than Kira. According to William, this was more of a drop-in kinda place for those who needed some time out. Witches had problems too, apparently.

'William asked me to let you know he is taking Azrael down to the horses,' Greta said. She had a little pug nose, an upturn at the tip that made her look as if she were sniffing something foul.

'Again?' Kira said. 'Didn't they just get back?' Christ, Az had a major hard-on for equines.

'No. They did not.' Greta's solemn brown eyes took in Caleb and Kira. 'You may have been too preoccupied in your game to notice. He has been watching TV for several hours. Vail has been pretending to purchase jewellery items for him on the shopping channel.'

'Do you have a problem with men wearing tiaras, Greta?' Kira said. She didn't need this smug little cow reminding her of the fact that she'd ignored Az for a few hours. She needed some time out from those sad, lost eyes.

Greta toyed with the string on her peasant top. Even Kira, keen to dislike every part of the sullen chick, had to admit she had a great set of boobs. 'He is not a man, Kira. Even you are surely able to recognise that.'

And Kira wanted to tear those tits off that pompous, condescending chest. 'I recognise that you are a –'

Caleb laughed, a rumble that came from deep inside his deliciously hairy chest, and put his hand on her shoulder. Kira's anger nose-dived. It was impossible to hear that sound and stay pissed off. Jesus, the guy was some kind of laugh wizard. Was that even a thing?

'Everyone is a little tense,' Caleb said. 'I'm going to get the evening meal started. And then perhaps we should line up some massages for after the ceremony?'

His spell even seemed to work on pug-face. Greta gave him a small smile and nodded. 'Yes. I've chosen a time for the ceremony, too. That's also what I came to tell you. The moon will align at nine, the time of its greatest strength, so the ceremony will commence then. William hopes we might be finished with the meal before then?'

Kira thumped the pestle against her metal hand. Moon will align? Oh for crying out loud.

'Of course,' Caleb said. 'Please let William know Kira will assist me.' He gave her a lopsided grin. 'I will keep her out of trouble until then.'

But Greta didn't seem interested in Kira or the trouble she was keeping out of, leaving the room without another word. Caleb placed the mortar on the bench and gestured to a stool. 'Don't look so frightened, Kira –'

'I'm not scared.' Words like whiplash.

'I know. I said frightened. There can be a difference. Azrael will not be harmed. You have William's word. Greta is very capable, and despite her demeanour, very kind. Now here, pound these peppercorns for me.'

Meal prep took longer than expected. It was almost nine by the time they'd settled on thick cushions around a low set table in the converted barn, and stuffed themselves stupid with an array of noodles. Decent conversion too, Kira would give them that. Burgundy walls, thick wooden beams gleaming under lights that looked as if they'd been woven from a bunch of twigs. Caleb the chef needed the goddamn Nobel Peace Prize for chefery. The man could do Singapore noodles like no one's business. But the wine situation was a human-rights violation. What kind of a fucking coven had no wine? A long, wet string of cold noodle hit Kira square in the face.

'Jesus, Az. Stop playing with your food.' She snatched the bamboo chopsticks from his hand, flinging them onto the table. Vail's shoulders jiggled. 'Are you laughing at me, you little shit?'

Bark definitely worse than bite, but hey, it was fun to see Leona glower when she thought Kira was dissing her little boy.

Vail grinned at Kira as if she were some rainbow-pooping unicorn. He shook his head, cheeks full with the effort of not making a sound. Kind of cute really. If he was lucky, he might grow up to be remotely attractive. Someone not so cute, though, was Greta. Face framed by rusty-red hair, she stacked the empty bowls but kept her gaze on Kira.

'I'm pretty fucking gorgeous, right?' Kira leaned back on her hands and stuck out her not-so-ample chest. Blake got those goods. What a waste. It was highly unlikely her uptight sister even masturbated, let alone fucked anyone else. 'Do you like what you see?'

'I don't know what I see,' Greta said. Steady as you like. Not batting a barely visible sandy-coloured eyelash.

'What's that supposed to mean?'

'An oblivious drunken slut, or a frightened and very lost soul.'

Leona, freshly washed hair plastered to her head, sucked in an audible breath. Kira didn't shift from where she lounged against the cushions. This wasn't her first insult rodeo. Generally, every night out had one. And she'd had a lot of nights out.

'I'm an enigma. Want to explore me?'

'Yes. I do.'

Vail coughed on his green tea. Azrael poked his finger into a piece of something pale, pink, and sticky on one of the central platters.

'Your edges are jagged, Kira,' Greta said. 'You do understand that, don't you? There is emptiness where there should be substance.'

A retort died on Kira's tongue, and something cold raked through her. Greta's gaze held her. Looked right into her. As though she could see the actual cavity where Kira's metal heart lay. The bitch was right. She was empty. Had been since the moment she'd woken up sans Dad, heart, and arm.

For crying out loud. What kind of fucking coven didn't have wine?

'Greta, that will do.' William's voice remained warm and silky. 'She has endured enough.'

'I can see that,' Greta said, so softly Vail leaned forward, face all screwed up. Clearly wanting to know more. But it was time to end whatever the hell this session was.

'Okay, well that was fun.' Kira got to her feet, using Az's shoulder as leverage. 'We doing this seance thing or what? Thought you guys were going to try to work out where numpty-no-nuts here is from or something?' She ruffled Az's hair. Damn. Just like the real thing. He uncrossed his legs and moved to follow. It really was like having your very own super-hot puppy.

'Yes. Absolutely.' William handed Caleb a stack of bowls. 'Thank you, Caleb. Delightful as always. Now, if everyone would follow me, please.'

He ushered them into a secondary room, smaller than the main dining area and strewn with cushions. Apparently no one believed in chairs here. Kira spotted a couple of beanbags and made a beeline for the retro print one in the far corner. Which meant Azrael did, too. He tilted his head as he watched her sit down. Then he lowered himself into the lavender-coloured bag beside hers, his body going rigid at the scrunching sound that followed.

'It's okay.' Vail smiled at him from a pile of patchwork cushions. 'There's little beads inside it . . . beans . . . but not real beans. It's comfortable, isn't it?'

Azrael glanced from the bag to Vail three times before he answered. 'Yes. It is comfortable.'

The walls were hung with a couple of landscape prints. The type of hangings you find in those chain stores that have all the furniture you build yourself. Kira didn't know what she expected in a coven, maybe some eyes of newt, or bats, or something.

William sat in front of Azrael, trying to explain to Az what was going to happen. But the horse-loving demon was more interested in poking his fingers into the beans.

'Hey, Az. Come on. Pay attention.' Kira tapped her foot against his. 'Be a good boy. You want to find out what's going on, right?'

Sea-green eyes rested on her. Pale pink lips pressed closed. Kira held out her hand, the skin and bone one, and he rested his own in her palm without hesitation. Yeah. She got it. She wasn't so sure she wanted to dig around in this one, either. Christ, her belly churned. The food was good. Fucking great actually. It wasn't food doing the churning. It was pure, cold nerves.

'Hurt him and I'll do bad things to your kaftan,' she said.

William nodded, giving her a gentle smile. Greta padded barefoot into the room, sitting on Azrael's left beside where Vail crouched. Leona squeezed herself into the narrow space behind Azrael, her back up against the white-washed stone of the wall. Last to arrive to the party was the lizard, who'd been noticeably absent during dinner, but Kira had drawn the line at why a reptile had skipped on the noodles. Now Bradley scurried up Vail's back and perched himself on his right shoulder.

'Great, the whole gang is here,' Kira declared.

'We will need to touch you, Azrael.' William spoke slowly, as if Az needed time to lip-read. 'Do not be afraid. If you do not wish to proceed, we will cease immediately.'

Az remained silent, looking at each of them in turn before turning to Kira.

'You're good, buddy. I'm a black belt. I've got this.' She owned multiple black belts – Gucci, Versace – so it wasn't entirely a lie. And it was enough for Az. He settled into his beanbag, holding firmly to Kira's hand.

Everyone rested fingertips against various parts of Az's body: his arms, his shoulders, for William it was his feet. Bare. As everyone's were. No shoes in the barn.

Chanting started next. At some point someone had lit a bundle of herbs over near the doorway. A curling line of smoke meandered into the room, bringing with it a pungent, bitter smell. Almost as bad as the bunch of twigs Az had been holding when Kira had awoken in the car. She crinkled her nose and held her breath. The sing-song continued, building in volume. Greta had a surprisingly melodic voice. In fact, in other circumstances, Kira could have drifted off to sleep to it. The words were foreign, but she couldn't place the language at all. At times she thought she caught Swedish, then there'd be a sentence that might have been Japanese. All in all, it sounded like gibberish. And after ten minutes of it, nothing much happened. Kira stifled a yawn. She and Az were the only ones with their eyes open. Even Bradley had his beady balls covered up. The vapour from the burning herbs filled the room with a light haze, and the scent altered into something more pleasant. Like a fresh-cut lawn.

It took Kira a moment to work out why Vail's cheeks suddenly caught the light. Tears. Seriously?

Bradley opened his eyes, long candy-floss tongue slipping up over one dark eyeball, and Leona slumped forward, head down, her almost-dry hair falling across her face. Kira narrowed in on Az, who seemed the least affected by whatever was going on. A little forlorn perhaps, but that was stock-standard with him. Greta began to shiver. Not just a little bit of a chill but an I've-been-stuck-in-a-fucking-freezer kind of shudder. Tiny gasps escaped her. William opened his eyes. He frowned but kept his fingers on Az. Next second, Greta's shivers turned into something more like an epileptic fit. Her body spasmed, jerked forward, head snapping up and down. But she didn't take her hand from where it rested on Az's arm.

'What the fuck is happening?' Kira gripped Az's hand harder. But if whatever was going down was hurting him, he didn't show it.

'One moment, Kira,' William said, eyes locked on Greta.

Her head flew back, mouth wide open. The cry that left her sat halfway between agonised and *I've just come*.

She slumped to one side, her hand slipping from Az. Now William sprang into action, gathering her in his arms. Gentle fingers brushed back the auburn strands stuck to her damp forehead.

'By the Maiden's graces.' Leona stared at Azrael, wide-eyed. 'How do you live with such pain?'

His grasp on Kira's hand tightened. 'Pain?'

'What are you talking about?' Kira looked between the tan-queen and the collapsed redhead. 'Someone want to fill me in?'

Christ almighty, everyone looked as though they'd been shat on by the devil himself. Even the reptile.

Vail wiped at his damp cheeks. 'We know who he is. And he's been in terrible, painful darkness for a very long time.'

'I don't understand . . . .' Kira shook her head. 'Who is he?'

'Enkidu.' Greta's suddenly gravelly voice was sex-line ready. 'His name is Enkidu.' She leaned against William.

'Okay.' Kira swallowed. 'Well sorry, Az, but that name sucks. So we're sticking with Az. Is that all you got?'

'It is all we needed.' Even Leona's fake tan seemed faded. 'There is no doubt now. The old gods stir again in this world. But how is this possible, how can you be here? You have been dead for thousands of years. What in all the Maiden's graces is going on in that place?'

Az's grip grew uncomfortable, but Kira wasn't ready to let go. 'Gods? Right. Sure. Look, you're saying his Enkidoodle name like I should know what it is. Do you recognise it, Az? Do you know that name?'

His eyes didn't fix in one spot, moving around the room as though he expected the answer to be pinned to the whitewashed wall somewhere. 'No. I do not know that name.'

The faintest whinny of one of the horses filled the temporary silence. Vail was first to speak.

'Have you heard of the Epic of Gilgamesh?'

'Is it a movie?' Kira said.

Vail shrugged, and Leona tut-tutted.

'I'm not sure,' Vail said. 'It's a super-famous story; some consider it the first great work of literature. It came out of ancient Mesopotamia, where the Sumerians were –'

Kira sighed. 'Right. Those guys again.'

Almond eyes solemn, Vail nodded. 'Yes. The epic is about one of the great kings. His name was Gilgamesh, obviously. He was supposedly a demigod himself, but whatever the truth of that might be, he was an actual king. There is documented history of him.'

The names got better and better. Kira wiped at her nose; the tip was icy cold. No one interrupted Vail and he continued.

'Story goes that he wasn't doing such a great job ruling his people. He was arrogant and cruel. So the goddess of creation, Aruru, sent a creature, a being called Enkidu, to try to balance things out. Enkidu was a force of nature, a wild man. Scholars who study the myth think was he was meant to represent a countervailing force to everything Gilgamesh represented: civilisation and the strength of man. But Gilgamesh was determined to tame Enkidu, any way he could. He used a woman first to tempt him –'

'Hey, good for you, Az.' Kira patted Az's knee. If any of this was ringing any bells, they weren't in Az's head. He sat with head lowered, his expression hidden.

Vail's face reddened, but he kept on, peering down at his sneaker laces. 'Anyway, eventually Gilgamesh and Enkidu met, they wrestled, and Gilgamesh won – civilisation overcoming nature – but they became really good friends. *Really* good friends, according to some interpretations. Inseparable. And a formidable team.'

'Sure, I get it. A story. Symbolic.' Kira rocked back on her heels. Her left foot tingled with pins and needles. 'But what you're trying to tell me is that the wild man from some ancient bedtime story is this guy? I mean, seriously, come on. How are you even getting this name?'

'From his head,' Leona said. 'Same way we got Kur and utukku from those possession spirits, only Az . . . Enkidu was much harder to decipher.'

Bradley chirruped, giving his reptilian stamp of approval.

'And what does his head say he's doing here?' Sure. Let's go with this. *Jesus Christ, Blake. How deep in shit are you?*

Greta shifted, supporting herself with one hand braced against the floor. 'I don't know. What I do know is a living being exists inside that metal shell, one from a different time. But I couldn't see any more. The thoughts are fractured. Damaged maybe? I don't know. Anything more than his name and his pain are unreachable. It's like trying to hold on to a mist.'

Kira chewed at the dry skin on her bottom lip. It was probably a great time to tell them about the whole fireworks-on-contact thing. But the words just wouldn't come.

William picked at a little golden bump of thread on the midriff of his kaftan. His nails needed a clip desperately. 'But his arrival may account for the strengthening of our abilities. He is a creature of nature, a powerful force of wildness. It's possible our Maiden's time actually began with him, a by-product from when the gods first put him on this Earth. And until now, she has not known her full strength.'

Leona scratched at the side of her head, strands bundling into a nest over her ear. 'It would explain the hotel,' she glanced at Vail, 'and the arrival of those possession spirits. The strength of your cast.'

Vail refocused on his laces. 'Perhaps. It doesn't change the outcome, though.'

Leona tilted her head from side to side, her neck cracking, seeming to shrug off his lament. 'And the woman in the Maserati. Suffice to say, she was not just a lost driver.'

Nina. Kira studied her bare feet, tracing her finger over the last speck of blue nail polish on her big toenail. 'I knew her.'

'You what?' Leona rose up on her high horse. 'And you failed to say something? Are you completely –'

White witch wasn't making it easy to come clean.

'Insane?' Kira glared. At her, and Greta. 'Sure. Oblivious slut? Absolutely. I fuck . . .' She glanced at Vail who was beetroot red still, and just to top off the weirdness of the day, she couldn't bring herself to drop the f-bomb. 'I slept with her. Last year in

Greece. Now she turns up here. Any of you witches got any leg-of-frog stew that can decipher that one?'

Apparently not. Crickets. Despite Kira's valiant attempt to be not vulgar, Vail looked fit to burst into flame.

'It is indeed strange. She appeared aware of Azrael's . . . uniqueness?' William's ever-gentle tone made it a little easier to breathe.

Kira nodded. 'Yeah, she knew.' Nearly got decapitated by his uniqueness. This was that other point, the one where she told them about the wings. And the aliens. Kira cleared her throat, but those little nuggets of admission weren't going anywhere. An odd sense of guilt played at her. Her own sister had gone full-on Dr Frankenstein. That stung.

'She's probably been doing exactly what I've been doing. Watching the Facility.' Leona crossed her legs. 'Anyone with any lick of perception could tell something wasn't right in the place. She simply went for a soft, easy target.'

Lovely. Kira the easy target.

'I didn't fucking tell her anything.'

'She wasn't searching for words,' Vail said. 'It's not like that.'

'It's your smell,' Greta declared, upright now. 'You reek of it now having been with Enkidu, but I suspect you held a hint of it before then. A preternatural odour that clings to beings like him. And us.'

Perfect. Kira the *stinking* easy target.

She stood up, done with this space. 'Guys, this has been fun. If by fun I mean excruciatingly weird and unhelpful. Which I do. Let's just say, for kicks, that someone has burritoed the spirit of some ancient wild man into a three-million-dollar metal suit, I have one question for you. What the fuck did they do that for?' She raised her arms, and her eyebrows. 'Huh? Nothing? Nobody? Well, here's something for all the girls and boys, there are four more.'

Gotta give them something. Till Rossiter got here, this would do.

'Four more what?' Greta's pug nose worked overtime.

'Of him. Four more metal suits. They were working on four more. Az was some kind of test dummy, I think. They didn't give a rat's about him in the end. It's why we could get out of there.'

Leona's choice of curse words was, admittedly, quite impressive. But there was no time to hand out prizes. Azrael tried to get up. The press of his hand against the beanbag split the material and sent a white storm of beads cascading around his feet as he rose.

'I died,' Azrael said. 'You said I died. How did I die? What does your story say?'

A look passed between William and Greta. All at once Kira had the urge to brace, and a trickle of damn goosebumps marched up her flesh arm.

She edged in closer to Az. 'Hey, he asked you a question.'

Vail took the mic. 'Enkidu . . . he and Gilgamesh . . .'

'You two pissed off the gods,' Leona took over. 'Got too big for your britches. Gilgamesh even thought he could turn down the goddess of war, Inanna. And she didn't like it. Not one little bit. Decided to punish them . . . you . . . sent the Bull of Heaven to deal with you and your king. Only you killed the Bull. Dead as a dodo –'

'Good for you, Az,' Kira said. Adrenaline pumping as if she'd stolen a car.

'Not good.' Leona seemed to be enjoying the drama, dropping her voice low, looking out from beneath a mussed-up fringe. 'Not at all. The Bull was a god. And a married one at that. His wife didn't take it too well. None of the deities did. They gave you a right painful, slow death. Some kind of illness that went on for months and months to torment your lover. Your king. The story, till now, has always ended with you being very dead, Enkidu.'

Eron - 29

The evening's slumber had not been fluid, leaving Eron tossing and turning throughout the night, the foreign hum of the city beneath him reaching through the barrier of deep sleep more than once. He did not begrudge the interruption entirely. Agar had dwelled in his dreams, his presence heavy and unsettling.

Little different than he was now. Seated beside Eron in the white Range Rover, bulletproof panelling separating the driver from her backseat passengers. The entire vehicle was fortified to ensure that should Agar manage to override the inhibitors, and then somehow overpower Eron and the mea stone, the mobile enclosure would secure itself against its unruly inhabitant and encase the gallu in a tomb on wheels. Eron squinted into the late-morning sunshine. The predictors of weather had been accurate. The day was clear and bright. Multitudes of humans went about their mundane daily tasks, and Eron stifled the low ripple of longing that ran through him.

'One minute until arrival, sir.'

Eron acknowledged the driver with a nod.

He glanced at his reflection in the tinted window. A pair of eyes, dreadfully plain brown, stared back at him. His long silver hair was braided and tucked up under a black cap with a red logo on the front. A music band. One he'd heard of, but he kept that knowledge to himself. Mentioning it would only draw attention to his time beyond Facility walls. With a pair of tight faded jeans, a white long-sleeved T-shirt with an advertisement for a soda on the front, and heavy-soled black boots, he was, so far as he was concerned, remarkably unimpressive to anyone glancing his way. He slid on a pair of black sunglasses and patted his waist, feeling the press of the margate fixed in its holster. It was similar in ways to the Taser used by humans, though the margate would melt internal organs if Eron desired such a result. He moved his attention to the two bracelets clinging to his right wrist, edging them away from the bony joint there. One was a simple inhibitor bracelet. But the other, a Telteriun cuff, was much more.

He was ready. Though his pulses, all out of sync, suggested otherwise.

The vehicle drew to a stop on the second level of a car park, affording them a view of the starting point of the parade. Further down the road, organisers tried valiantly to control the vast array of vehicles and humans lining up in wait for the go-ahead to begin their movement through the city. The costumes and vehicles being guided into the town square, where the parade would begin, were a veritable rainbow of colours and elaborate designs. A sky of perfect clear blue hung over them, the sun perched high above the skyscrapers. The crowds were already at a considerable thickness alongside the road, exuberant, vocal specimens.

Oblivious.

Eron took a moment to regulate his breathing before he triggered the Bind. Wishing to make a point, he decided against subtlety and was rewarded when Agar jerked, head snapping back like a sleeper doused with ice-cold water. The ricochet shuddered through Eron's bones, but he did not so much as blink.

'Let us go,' he said.

Agar's expression remained unaffected, but the swell of something rancid pulsed through the connection. They stepped out of the car, Agar following with lazy obedience down the stairs and out onto the street. Civilian clothes did little to quench the overbearing presence of the gallu. His carapace managed to block the light no matter where one stood beside him. Eron quickened his stride, desirous of a few paces of distance. But he took no more than a handful of steps before slowing. The throng of humans ahead of him was a denser group than any he'd been in before, including the places Kira had taken him. And she was not present this time to control the situation, to aid him in blending in. Eron pushed a strand of hair behind his ear, adjusted his cap, and recentred himself.

The parade would follow a brown-watered river that snaked right through the city centre, concluding at a large oval stadium on the city's east side. According to Clara, the stadium normally hosted sporting events, but today it would serve as an enormous concert venue. With part of the field being utilised as a stage, the rest was standing room for those wishing to dance. There was the possibility that occupancy would exceed a hundred thousand humans. Here at the commencement area, thunderous music already beat out from a sound system.

The scent of the mass of humanity clung to Eron's nostrils, overwhelming after so long isolated. He fought to keep his face devoid of any discomfort, but Agar made it difficult, tugging and teasing at the connection with all the gentleness of a cluster of Serifax, the irksome scavengers of Syrana's Telho Plains.

They halted ten metres from the start of the procession line. Clara had been correct in her deduction Eron would not stand out here. He had been to places such as this before: some of Kira's favoured places of amusement. He'd revelled, as she'd said he would, in that rare place where humans broke from the rigidity of gender obsession, turning it upside down and inside out. Dressing as they pleased.

'Thirty minutes till we get this party started,' the announcer declared, voice booming through shuddering speakers.

Eron's fingers pressed upon the indents in the cuff. Access granted. Every tiny pulse in his body hammered out of time. He stood on one side of something momentous. Something he'd feared for a time he would not be part of. Now he hesitated. His fingers hovered. Commands went uninitiated. Around him the scents and heat and sounds of the humans coursed through every inch of his world: the flutter of long blonde hair, the high pitch of laughter, a belch from an overweight man drinking a beer, and a screech from a gangly girl child. Who amongst them would fall, once Eron released one of the Four on this unprepared battlefield?

Agar's head tilted, his smoky-grey eyes fixed on Eron. Something resembling a smile curled at thin lips, and Eron saw he had been wrong to compare this gallu to a mere scavenger. Agar was the Precon beast itself, their Lord Lahar's totem creature. A beast that feasted on the cruelty of the hunt, not the necessity.

A woman of advanced years brushed past Eron, excusing herself with a smile.

'Sorry, sweetheart.' She looked up at him, as most humans tended to require. A frown added more wrinkles to her face. 'Oh . . . oh dear . . . goodness, you're one of them, aren't you?'

All his pulses seemed to still.

Her younger companion grabbed her arm, pulling her away. 'I'm so sorry.'

As they edged away, the older woman continued to peer at Eron. 'Gosh, I really can't tell if it's a boy or a girl. Incredible. What do you think? I couldn't see an Adam's apple. Do they get them removed –'

'Nan, you promised you wouldn't do this.' Her escort threw Eron another apologetic glance.

Releasing his held breath, Eron instigated final protocol and pressed his fingers upon the hexagons etched into the onyx cuff. Blake, Cym, and the other engineers had laboured over this system for some time. The relief on Blake's face when the design had held up under testing with Azrael was amongst only a handful of decipherable expressions Eron had witnessed take shape there.

Agar shifted his broad shoulders as minute vents opened in various sections of the carapace. These openings allowed the barest hint of Agar's core, his essence, to be released into his faux vascular system. It waited there, close to the surface. Accessible to touch and absorption. Sensing the release, Agar's fists clenched. A tremor ran through his solid body. Eron drew on the mea stone, holding firmer to Agar lest he decide his mission had begun. One more part of the process remained. Eron blinked, his gaze resting on Agar's bare right arm. No sign yet that the release had begun. The gallu wrestled against the Bind, and his resistance bounced against the inside of Eron's skull like pinpricks.

Then, there it was.

A sight hidden to all those around them, but revealed to Eron via the contacts he wore. Tiny veins of brilliance coursing through Agar's skin.

Now it could begin. Eron released Agar. *Go.* The command seared down the Bind, heated and sharp. But his show of strength was wasted. Agar didn't need any goading. He strode away and plunged into the crowd.

'Shit.' Eron jogged to catch up, but in truth it would be hard to lose the gallu. It was like running after a tiny sun. Agar's true core radiated around him, an aura Eron could not miss. Each human he passed by, every arm he touched, every shoulder he bumped, now wore a smudge of that same radiance. There was a reason the humans had dubbed these gallu the Four Horseman of the Apocalypse in their ancient tales. These beings truly were harbingers of destruction and death. Toxic to mortals.

Divine biological weapons.

All humans who came in contact would suffer in some way, but before the construction of the carapaces most would have perished. Now, with the protective layer of Telteriun between mortal and gallu, it would only be the weak, the vulnerable who would succumb when contaminated. But the carapaces were not built as a safety shield for the humans. They were built to prolong the gallus' stay on Earth. As a human in space required a suit, so did the gallu require protection here. A place no longer rich with the sustaining influence of the gods.

As toxic as the gallu may be to humans, they would not fell a demi-god such as Dumuzi. An immortal. And when the radiance came in contact with his human shell, the impact would blaze like a beacon.

Agar shouldered past a man who rivalled him in size. The bald-headed man turned, a blaze of anger reddening his face. Agar placed a hand on the man's shoulder. Eron braced. Again, unnecessary. The human's face softened at the edges, the harsh lines crumpling. Eron had witnessed that look before. Television had taught him much. When humans saw baby animals, or indeed baby humans, this was the expression that took them. The Four were toxic in more ways than one; the were masters of manipulation who could influence their prey. Lull them into subservience.

Agar released his captive and moved on. The bald man greeted a group of friends, shaking each one's hand in turn, and the radiance slipped upon new hosts. Eron's world grew brighter with its expansion.

A young man, clad in vibrant floral prints and crystal-embedded sunglasses that sparkled in the sunshine, wrapped his free arm around Agar. Eron clenched his fist, readying himself. Death or injury in a crowd such as this would only hinder the mission. But intervention was again unnecessary. Agar wrapped a solid arm around the man's torso. The young man let out a cheer that melted into the mutterings of the crowd and the thumping music. His shoulders glowed with radiance. Dancing with abandon, he grabbed the woman beside him, an acquaintance judging by what followed. They pressed lips and bodies together. And so the radiance rested upon her as well. At this rate, the gallu's touch would spread far and wide within the hour.

Someone collided with Eron, and a dull pain moved through his foot. A bright pink stiletto heel rested on the tip of his steel-capped boot.

'Sorry.' A woman pressed up against him, gazing up at him with dilated pupils. She had not, he suspected, yet returned home from her evening activities. Much like a good portion of the group surrounding Eron. Her long curling blonde hair rested on top of ample breasts straining against a strapless top. Radiance gleamed from the crevice between her mammary glands. 'Isn't this the best? Fucking brilliant, huh?'

Eron glanced away. 'Indeed.'

He tried to detach her, but she clung to him, raising one hand and edging his cap back, toying with a strand of his hair.

'Oh god, I love this colour. Dance with me, gorgeous.' Her hands slipped down towards the belt of his jeans. Eron's clothing was far too tight, but he'd had to make do with what was supplied. Her hands slipped under his shirt, nearing the margate strapped there. Eron stepped away and bumped up against a thin man with spiked purple-tinted hair.

'Want a swig?' He held up a silver oval container. 'This will make you feel better.'

Eron shook his head. He hadn't touched a drop of alcohol since that final night with Kira beyond Facility walls. Was never likely to if there was any chance his head would pound again that way. The man shrugged and took a deep gulp himself. Moving deeper into the crowd, Eron was jostled past a couple doing a rather wild dance that involved dipping the woman in an uncomfortable-looking bend. On the parade route everything sparkled and glistened, vibrant and loud and chaotic. Eron edged his way through the throng, headed for the glare of light up ahead that was Agar. Only the very top of Agar's head was visible to him. A hand patted Eron's buttocks; he ignored it and moved on. Though the proximity of so many, so close, was unsettling to begin with, Eron adjusted faster than he'd imagined he could. Enjoying it, if he were honest with himself. Younger children sat atop their adults' shoulders, waving to the assembled performers. Eron breathed in the heavy waft of the humans around him: perfumes, body odours, heated air, and the tang of sweaty skin. Though his movement was impeded by the press of bodies, Eron had never moved more freely. He let his fingers brush against those he moved with. Felt the contrasts in the fabrics and the skins they wore.

Then Agar was right before him with one arm draped over a man with a lined, attractive face, the other around the waist of a short black-haired woman in jeans and a bikini top. Agar had lifted her off her feet, her bare toes dangling over the grass. Eron couldn't make out her face because it was blocked by Agar's own. The pair was locked in a kiss. There was nothing gentle about Agar's movements, he ground his face against the woman's, forcing her neck back at an awkward angle. They pulled apart, and the woman let out a cry. Painless. A grin was smeared on her face, barely visible beneath the glare of radiance that covered her flesh. Agar set her on the ground and turned to the man. No hesitation from either gallu or human. Lips pressed together again in a manner that made Eron wince, certain human teeth would be broken. Some in the crowd goaded them. A palpable energy hummed from the small circle. Agar pulled away, and the man staggered, a smile blazing across his face. The radiance lifted from him, rising in the air in small delicate tentacles that corkscrewed into the surrounding crowd. The male and female grasped each other, pressing against each other as though desperate to merge as one. Eron's memory of his own body moving in such a way rose up to taunt him. He shut it down, burying it, lest Agar catch hold and use it against him.

'Holy crap, man,' a man shouted at Agar. 'What are they on? I want a bag of it.'

Agar didn't reply, glancing at Eron as he moved away. He raised his wide hands, letting them brush over the moving bodies.

Eron struggled to gather his thoughts over the top of the screeching speaker system. The crowd seemed to recognise the music being played, and the bodies around him erupted into a spirited dance. He was jostled from one side to another as he followed after Agar. More than one stray hand pressed against his body. More than one proposition was uttered. The air grew thick, the atmosphere weighing down on him. And over it all, the radiance spread. The toxin finding its way deeper and deeper into the masses.

Kira - 30

Kira lay spread-eagled on the massage table, her hair slicked to her face and her breath coming in short, sharp bursts. The air reeked of sweat and other nasty stuff. A salty tang so heavy you could lick it. Her metal heart was the quietest thing about her. Skin tingled, nerves rang. The hum of an orgasm drifted through her. Her masseuse was a gobsmacked huddle in a cane chair beside the French doors. Caleb sat there, naked and damp, head tilted back against the chair and that crazy, mesmerising smile plastered on his face. Last night he'd been wearing socks with his sandals, but she'd forgiven the style crime about five seconds after he'd knelt between her legs. They'd both come back for seconds this morning, and here they were two hours later.

'How about now?' Caleb cupped his fingers around his beard. 'Did I get that knot out of your back this time?'

'Give me five minutes. I'll let you know.'

'Well, make it a quick five minutes. I need to go and start preparing lunch.' A lopsided grin took years off his face but she guestimated he was mid-forties. Almost double her age, just the way she preferred. Bugger the fumbling bullshit of the newbie. Kira sat up and nearly slid off the vinyl table. The towels Caleb had put down when he had actually been giving her a massage were piled under the table, in need of a wash. Like she was. Kira sighed, a long breath that went all the way to the bottom of her lungs. Chef knew how to use his utensils and had taken her to that place she hunted for. That little island of oblivion that came when she did.

Their view opened out onto a wide veranda, heavy-hung with grape vines, nothing but rolling hills and a narrow river running off towards some mountains in the distance. Picture postcard stuff, but hard to give two craps about when King Kong was between your legs. William said sexual energy was as natural as any other. If so, Caleb must have been that Maiden chick's favourite witch.

'Well, that was nice.' Kira wiggled into her G-string and contemplated the effort it was going to take to drag her skin-tight pants over the sweat coating her. A bath was definitely in order. 'Might want to open the doors. I think we've made this room funky.'

Caleb's smile dazzled her again, white teeth showing, rounded stomach and man-boobs jiggling with his laughter. He swung open the French doors. 'See you at lunch.'

He grabbed her ass, then left her alone.

Picking up the least offensive towel, Kira rubbed at her armpits. At some point during the massage, before the actual fucking part, someone had dropped off some clothes. Might have been Greta, Kira couldn't be sure. She'd been face down, ass up. Whoever it was had left a pair of faded denim jeans, and a grey Under Armour t-shirt. Sportswear didn't do it for her, but the thought of dragging on her bandage top again kind of made her gag. Footsteps pounded along the veranda. If Caleb thought he was getting a third helping, he would be sadly disappointed.

'Kira? Kira?'

To be fair, Vail got to the wide-open doors before she had a chance to reach for the shirt, but she could have lifted the towel to cover herself. It was an option. But it was way more fun to fuck with him.

'Yes, Vail?'

'Oh god.' He covered his face, spinning round. 'I'm so sorry.'

'You've seen tits before, surely.'

'Maybe. I'm not really...they're not my thing. Particularly. I'm pretty sure.'

Christ, she was an A-class bitch sometimes. 'Sorry, dude. Didn't mean to –'

'It's all right, Kira,' Vail said, soft, as though he were soothing a baby off to sleep. 'I know you are upset and confused. You think it's safer to keep your distance.'

Oh hell no. A sixteen-year-old K-pop reject did not get to shrink her. She paid very good money for that kind of stuff.

'If you didn't want a peep show, what do you want, Vail?'

With his back to her still, he lifted his hand, brandishing a small black flip-top phone. 'Rossiter has sent William a text. He's here. Leona is going to pick him up.'

It would probably scar the kid for life, but she couldn't help herself. Kira raced up behind him, tits flapping in the breeze, and wrapped her arms around him. 'Thank fuck.'

Vail giggled like a preschooler, but didn't try to pull away.

Now that the big man was here, maybe this whole shit show might make some sense.

Kira paced back and forth across the top of the driveway, glancing at her watch. Thirty minutes. How long did it take to find the enormous man? She pressed her hands to her face. Leona was driving. It was going to take for fucking ever. Maybe these witches could cure Kira of her car-driving thing, make her forget all about the body in the passenger seat and the smell of burning, 'cause this was just getting to be a pain in the ass.

On William's direction, Rossiter had dumped his car outside of Jackson and now waited in some old derelict factory. Leona would take another route back to the farmhouse, as well as use an indifference incantation to ward off potential witnesses. Just like she'd apparently done at the hotel. It was like being stuck in a warped Bond movie. Ridiculous. Hocus-pocus bullshit.

'Fuck!' Kira shouted to the clear late-morning sky.

'You've done that already. All night,' Greta called from where she perched on the edge of the veranda.

Azrael stood off to one side, glancing between the horses in the lower paddock and Kira. Az, Enkidu. Whoever the hell he was. She hadn't spent much time with him since the whole seance reveal thing.

'Didn't want you to be disappointed in me, seeing as you have me all worked out,' Kira snapped.

Greta tossed her head, flicking off the comment as if it were an irritating gnat.

'There!' Vail jumped up and down.

A tiny spot of blue was turning off the main road, about to begin the winding drive up the hill to the farmhouse. Before she knew what she was doing, Kira was running. She hadn't run in years, avoided it at all costs, but there was a goddamn fire under her feet today.

'Stay within the wardings. You stink, remember.' Greta's words washed away in the wind that meandered around the hill.

Kira's mad dash morphed into a stumbling fast walk. The road wasn't paved, and her sneakers slid easily on the loose gravel. She also wasn't entirely sure what the hell she was doing here, halfway down the hill, in the middle of the narrow road. Leona was just as likely to run her down as to stop for her. It was fifty-fifty.

Around the next bend she came face-to-face with the beat-up Datsun. The frown on Leona's face was visible from ten paces away. She honked the horn, as though Kira were a duck or cow she wanted to clear off the road. But she stopped the car at least. The rust-streaked thing rumbled its nuts and bolts but stayed put. Rossiter stepped from the car, and Kira had to wonder how the fuck he'd gotten himself into it in the first place. The guy could block out the sun. The bald dome he called a head just cried out for a rubbing, like the belly of a good luck Buddha. And shit, her eyes hurt. Must have been the dust.

They stood there. Staring at one another. Neither moving to do any more than raise a quick hand in greeting.

'Big man,' Kira said.

'Kira,' Rossiter said.

'I was just out for a run. Didn't realise you were coming.'

'Good to see you too, Kira.'

Leona pulled up close to the manicured garden that ran the circumference of the farmhouse. Well inside the wardings, Kira assumed. Safe inside that invisible curtain that supposedly hung over this place, thanks to the bundles of sticks and bat brains the witches had scattered round the property. Vail insisted no bats were involved, but Kira didn't believe him. All in all, it sounded like a very low-tech version of the Lucentshield that encased the Facility. And there, like here, she didn't know exactly what it was guarding against.

Rossiter unfolded himself from the car again, looking hard at Azrael, who had moved down to his horsey friends. Eron would have gone apeshit over the animals, too. Kira squeezed her eyes shut, the randomness of the thought catching her off guard. She opened her eyes. Rossiter's forehead bunched with lines.

'What ya thinking there, oh great guard of a body?' Kira kicked at a random stone. They weren't exactly best buds. She'd probably only spoken to him sober a handful of times, but damn if it wasn't good to see the big bastard.

'I'm wondering what the hell I'm involved in.' A muscle in his jaw flexed. Then he turned to her. 'Are you all right, Kira?'

'Life is pretty messed up, I'll be honest. What is going on in there, R-man? These loonies are trying to convince me that my sister sent me out into the world with some nature-loving, king-fucking ancient god—'

'No. Not a god, but created by them.'

Kira and Rossiter turned in unison to see William, resplendent in a fresh new kaftan. This one was cream with gold trimming and a low V-neck. Delightful.

'Rossiter, this is the head loony. William . . .' She had no idea of the guy's surname.

William did a little half bow. 'You are most welcome here, Rossiter. We have been waiting anxiously for you.' His gaze darted to Kira, and she wondered if he knew she'd been banging his chef while she waited anxiously. Not entirely sure what she thought of the idea that he might. Fuck, she was getting soft. 'Please, come and refresh yourself. I believe it's been a long journey.'

They headed up towards the house, Vail and Leona—clad in yet another fetching velour tracksuit, this one lime green— forming a procession behind them.

'Az, come on.' Kira waved, and like the good little wild-man demon he was, he trotted after her, one perfectly proportioned limb after the other. They strode down the hall, passing the doorway that opened into the kitchen. Caleb was bent over the stove, rounded face squinting with concentration. Kira whistled, drawing his attention, and darn if his crinkly old face didn't just light up when he saw her. A wink and then she was gone, moving on, and continuing down the length of the house and out to the converted barn. One side of it was all bi-fold doors, which were thrown open. Sunlight streamed in, glinting off the sequins on the piles of cushions and beanbags that seemed to have multiplied overnight. Bradley was perched on the low table they'd eaten off last night. The lizard stretched his scaly neck, craning to watch Rossiter's every move as he settled in one of two actual chairs that had appeared in the room, right beside the open doorways. He accepted the mug that Greta handed him.

'There will be food momentarily.' William eased himself down onto a beanbag, adjusting the kaftan folds around him. 'Was it a trouble-free journey?'

'If you're asking if anyone followed me, the answer is no.' Rossiter downed the entire contents of the mug and set it on the floor.

'I don't doubt your professionalism –'

'Jesus H. Christ, enough with niceties. What's with him?' Kira touched Az's sleeve. Someone had put Az in a T-shirt, super-snug fit. A vibrant green that made his eyes pop. 'Want to tell us what's going on?'

Rossiter picked up the empty mug, staring into its emptiness. 'This could be difficult to explain . . . considering certain confidential information.'

Kira was done with this shit. Waiting for Rossiter had clogged her up like a ninety-year-old in a nursing home. Time for verbal diarrhoea. 'Aliens. There's fucking aliens in the Facility.'

Greta cursed, and William's Adam's apple bobbed wildly.

'Aliens,' Vail echoed. All starry-eyed.

'Can I just say, I told you they were up to no good in there.' Leona spread her arms, orange face cracking with a wide smile. 'Did any of them listen to me? No.'

William raised his hands, kaftan fluttering. 'Now, now. Let's keep it down to a dull roar, shall we? Rossiter, we'd be most grateful if you could fill us in on some further details.'

'Well, I'd be most happy to.' The chair creaked under his weight as he rested one leg over the other. 'If I knew them. I've been instructed to protect an asset.' He gestured to Azrael, who stood beside Kira. 'To protect you too, Kira.'

'Great. Awesome. From what?'

'That part, I'm not clear on.'

Kira shoved her hands into the tangle of her curls. 'Then you're practically next to useless. Fuck.'

'Thank you, Kira. As pleasant as always.' Rossiter got out of his chair, pacing to the open doorway.

'Hard to be pleasant when people are dying around you. I know Blake's pissed about stuff, but she could have just asked me to leave the country. Not make me a target.'

'Now, now –' William said. 'Rossiter, please is there anything that might help us?'

Rossiter folded his tree-trunk arms. 'No offence, but I don't know who you are –'

Kira launched herself at Rossiter's back, using her metal fist to make a dent in the big man.

'Jesus!' Rossiter grabbed her wrists. 'What is wrong with you?'

'Me? What the hell is wrong with my sister? For god's sake, Rossiter, cut the shit and just tell us what you know. 'Cause I am going to lose my fucking mind.'

This is what happens when Kira doesn't get her special juice every day, people. Ability to deal, shrinks to nothing.

Rossiter pulled her hands against his chest. 'Hey, hey. It's okay, Kira.' His grip was gentle, and his tone dipped into Barry White territory. Kira stopped trying to scratch his heart out. 'You've done good. Really, really good. I'm sorry that Blake dumped you into this.'

What was with all the goddamn dust in this place? Someone buy the witches a vacuum cleaner. Kira tugged her hands free, and Rossiter turned his attention to William. 'The . . . aliens, came here some time ago. Blake told me that they'd been sent here by someone very powerful –'

'Gods tend to be powerful, so she got that right at least,' Leona sniffed.

Rossiter's smooth expression didn't shift. 'That the aliens are more advanced is undeniable, but whatever they wanted to do, they needed our help. Tamas invited Blake into the fold, and she went along with it –' He sought out Kira. 'The technology was incredible. It saved Kira's life. I believe Blake has felt a sense of obligation because of that.'

Sure, yeah. Let's go with that.

'She believes the aliens are looking for something – someone – here on Earth. The captain referred to the other carapaces as hunters. But there are only four. Not exactly an army. Blake didn't think –'

'No. She didn't at all. Just assumed she could mess with things beyond her.' Leona was becoming a great high-horse rider. 'Because that's what she's done. Messed with things. Who are they searching for?'

'She didn't give me details. But she's grown increasingly concerned that she may have –'

'Fucked up?' Kira said.

'Underestimated the cost of assisting the aliens in their mission.' Rossiter pulled a small rectangular box from a pocket on his leather jacket. The dullness of the metal matched that of Kira's arm. Telteriun. 'She told me that without Azrael, we're at a gunfight without a gun.'

If she was talking in dramatic metaphor, Blake was out of her fucking tree.

Rossiter tapped the box. 'And she gave me this. Said it had to be protected.'

Everyone gravitated towards him, human planets drawn to the sun. The box was plain, a single line carved into the rim.

He opened the lid.

'A rock?' Kira said. 'We're protecting a goddamn rock?'

Not even that. A pebble.

Bradley let out a squawk of astonishing magnitude, flinging himself off Vail's shoulder and hurtling towards Rossiter like a cold-blooded missile. The reptile was ninja-fast, and accurate, landing directly on the box. His tongue lashed out and stuck hard to the pebble. Rossiter swiped at the fleeing newt and missed. Bradley dropped to the ground, scurrying across the tiled surface, and clawing his way up Azrael's pant leg. The lizard was a blur of red and black across the dark material, up the traffic-light green shirt, and scampering his way up Az's neck. Meanwhile, in zombie town, Az didn't move. And still didn't move when Bradley flattened himself against his lips.

'Vail, control your reptile.' As Kira moved to swipe Bradley away, Az opened his mouth, and the lizard poked his head into the darkness. A second, no more, and then Bradley dropped away, flinging his little scaly body to the floor.

Another second later and Az began to choke, gagging so hard it sounded as if he might hurl almighty chunks any second. Something flew from his mouth, pinging against the tiled floor. Az let out a scream that tried to peel the paint off the walls. Kira flung her hands over her ears, clutching at her head. He doubled over and fell to his knees, guttural sobs replacing the ear-shattering scream.

'Az.' Kira landed on her knees beside him and, without thinking it through, grabbed his shoulders using both hands. Now it was her turn to scream. Her brain filled to bursting with sight and sound, both equally traumatic. She saw him. Truly saw him.

Enkidu.

His love for his king drove through her. They'd been masters of their world. Of each other. And it had pushed them too far. Too dangerously close to the gods. And Azrael suffered for it. Long and hard. Kira wanted to stop screaming, but it poured out of her as Azrael's true self poured *into* her. Someone was grabbing at her, trying to wrench her free. She felt their hands on her shoulders. A score of voices surrounded her, but she had become nothing but memory. Awful, breaking memory.

All at once she was free. The light flowed back in. Azrael stood in silhouette by the open doors, wings pluming from his back. He turned, and William dove to push Greta out of the way of the flailing blades of metal.

'Az, don't!' Kira cried.

But he did. Lifted off. And flew away.

Kira - 31

Kira dragged herself up the side of the hill, determined to make it look a hell of a lot easier than it was. The bump was barely entitled to call itself a hill, more like a soil pimple, but Christ, she might as well be hauling her ass through sticky toffee. Her body had felt like lead since Az's monumental breakdown nearly two hours ago, as though what she'd seen in his head had sapped everything from her. The afternoon sun was waning, which was nice because it was hot as shit out in the paddocks. And there hadn't be a single sign of the guy. Sweat beaded on Kira's top lip and her right armpit. One advantage of an entirely artificial arm: no stinky pit. She lifted her flesh arm and stuck her nose close. 'Oh god, that's nasty. Why didn't you tell me I stink like a monkey's ass?'

'I'm not familiar with the smell of a monkey's ass.'

Vail used a pair of binoculars to scan the area. William had headed east to scout the area there, while Greta, Leona, and everyone's favourite reptile, Bradley, remained at the ranch trying some witchy search techniques. Right now they were probably chanting round a pot of boiling frogs' brains and sheep dicks. All of them had declared she should stay at the ranch. And all of them believed she was resting in one of the bedrooms after her brain-freeze experience with Az. But Escape Tactics 101 were her bread and butter. Classic stuff. Pillows under the covers, all the usual shit. Rossiter was likely still sitting outside her room, guarding her. Poor dumb bastard. But if she had stayed indoors, that niggle of a panic attack would have exploded into something way more unattractive.

They were about five kilometres from the farm. Vail had nearly pissed himself when she'd popped up in the back seat of Leona's rust bucket, but he was putty in her hands, and it didn't take much to convince him to let her stay on the search. They'd driven down every country lane and along every dirt track they could find. Now they'd reached the head of a valley, paralleled by the low mountain range visible from the farmhouse. Green, green grasses of home stretched on as far as the eye could see.

'See anything?' Kira said. She shaded her eyes, looking for a tiny speck that might or might not be a flying angel up in the clouds. Assuming he was still flying. Could be hiding out in a barn somewhere, or long, long gone. Kira shifted her shoulders, tilting her head back and forth, trying to ease the stiffness there. Maybe she needed to get an actual massage next time.

'Nah. Don't think so. A helicopter heading east.' Vail turned, squinting into the sunlight. 'You okay? We can rest if you like.'

'Just because I don't feel the need to sprint up every incline we get to doesn't mean I need a rest, asshole.'

Vail did that thing, the suppressed smile that made him look ten times older than he was. The one that said he knew she was full of shit. Rossiter tried it too on the odd occasion. It generally just made the big guy look as though he needed to take a dump. And it also pissed her off. But not little Mr Bad Fringe. Vail was a different kettle of weird-ass fish. She wanted to plonk his scrawny ass down on this grassy knoll and just chill with him. Chat about shit. Chat about how shit things were. Tell him she was scared – about what might have happened to Blake and what was happening to Azrael. To her.

Vail sighed, lowering the binoculars. 'He could be anywhere.'

Kira slow clapped. 'First prize for amazing conclusions goes to . . . drum roll . . . the boy wizard.'

'Shut up.' Vail grinned, not in the least bit offended.

She checked for cow shit, then sat down. The grass was cropped down to nothing thanks to the black-and-white poop machines dotting the paddock around them. 'The guy has wings. He's probably in Thailand somewhere now, getting touched up by lady-boys, or boy-boys, or girl-girls. Drinking cocktails and snorting everything white he can get his hands on.'

Praise be to Jesus. Lucky bastard. Damn it was good to sit. Her ass was lead. She closed her eyes, the sunlight bright against her eyelids. The breeze was nice, if you liked air laced with manure.

'I don't think he'll go very far from you.'

Vail's voice made her jump, too busy sunning herself to realise he'd sat down beside her. Kira cleared her throat, bugged that it had crossed her mind how nice it would be to lay her head on his shoulder. Just for a minute. Just to rest a second. Give herself a mini time out from her own thoughts – and the godawful sting of Az's memories. She thought she knew what anguish was before. Fuck. No.

'If I were him,' she said, 'I'd keep running.'

Vail rocked onto his knees, pulling something from his jacket pocket. A jacket that was a size too big and an offence to human eyes. Denim, faded, but with patches of chequered material sewn at random over it. If Leona had bought it for him, or worse, made it, Kira would slap her.

'What did you see, Kira?' Vail reached for a nearby twig. 'I mean, if you feel ready to tell anyone . . .'

She let out a long, slow breath, watching Vail assemble his little voodoo pile. Sticks mostly, a couple of stones, and a few of those coins he liked to fling about and send people out of windows with. Channelled his focus, he said. Tuned him in to anything untoward that might be around. Preternatural. Supernatural. Az-natural. So far, everywhere they had stopped, he'd detected absolutely fuck all. Despite what Vail thought, it looked like Az did want to go very far from her.

'It's all pretty messed up.' She dug her fingertips against her temples, pressing too hard with metal. 'She hurt him pretty bad. Really bad.'

As if she were the devil herself kind of bad.

'Ereshkigal? You saw the goddess?'

'No, I didn't see anyone exactly. But that's the name I got, yeah.' It made her brain tingle, trying to explain it. 'I dunno, I just felt everything, knew stuff. He loved that Gilgamesh guy, I can tell you that for free. And not in the drinking-buddy kind of way.' She paused, swallowing. What had hit her hardest had been the sense of loss. The ache that had burrowed down so far into Az's psyche that it sucked at Kira even now. Quicksand at her feet. 'Leona was right . . . about him being in pain, all kinds of pain . . . I guess the old bat has some skills after all.'

Vail's smile was gossamer. So gentle her eyes stung. Kira dug her fingers into the earth. The metal registered the subtle temperature differences as her fingers went lower, sending the information directly to her brain. Top layer of earth was approximately eighteen degrees, cooler down lower.

The limb wasn't just pretty to look at, it was some super-fancy alien computer essentially. Hot wired into her brain. Brain-machine interface with extras, Blake told her. The 'extras' were the armadillo's ability to not only read her mind and do what she wanted—pick her nose, masturbate, mix a cocktail—but to read the world around her. Give her details, like how heavy an object was before she tried to lift it, or the temperatures around her. She didn't like to think too hard about what the inside of her skull looked like; if she was wired up or full of chips. Same went for her heart. What you didn't know didn't hurt you, right? Kira flicked her fingers, sending dirt spraying. She needed a drink. Water, actually. Throat dry as the Sahara. The very faint niggle of anxious butterflies still teased at her belly.

In terms of head fucks, this was up there. Azrael was this ancient dude, Enkidu. She knew it. She'd seen it.

'But what the hell is all this?' Kira tapped her metal fingers against her forehead. 'I mean, you said in the legend, that Epic of Gilgamesh thing, that the goddess killed Az. So not only is Enkidu fiction, he's dead fiction. And all because he killed some bull this goddess bitch liked or something?'

Vail finished assembling his little pile and carefully placed one last coin on the top of the pyramid-shaped assembly. 'Well, the Bull was actually –'

'You know what, I don't give a shit about the bull. This is fucking insane. Rossiter said the aliens called those other ones hunters. Hunting for fucking what? Az? I mean, has Blake dumped a live grenade in our laps?'

Placing his hands over the top of the little pile, Vail's eyes narrowed in focus. The coins rose up in the air, hovering just above his pyramid. 'I'm sorry, Kira. We were hoping that Rossiter had more details, but it seems your sister has kept him in the dark as well.'

She stared at the floating coins that caught the sun as they bobbed. Food would be good. Might stop the incessant churning of her belly. A change of topic would do in the meantime. 'Where's your mum, Vail? Your family? I mean, you're a kid. Just a kid.'

He glanced at her. 'My father has passed. Same as yours. But my mother, well, she's somewhere in Mongolia, last I heard. I haven't spoken to her in a very long time. Leona takes care of me. They were friends once.' The coins lowered back onto the pile. One of them slipped into the dirt. 'What about you? Your mum, I mean.'

Where the hell did the oxygen go? Were the motherfucking cows farting it out of existence? Kira pressed herself to her feet. As ungraceful as all hell, but she got there. 'Heart attack, when I was two. Didn't know her.'

Didn't know her sister, either, if it was time for honest confessions. And Dad was dead. So that pretty much made Kira a party of one. Even a fictional ancient dead dude had left her. Blake had asked her once what Kira liked so much about drinking. Well, this was fucking it. Liquid reality raincheck. Kira's hand shook. She clasped her metal fingers around her wrist.

'Kira, it's all right.' Vail took a step towards her. 'Look at me. Just take it easy.'

But the butterflies were morphing, growing claws and needlepoint beaks and jabbing at her insides. The anxiety monster raised its head, pushing its way into her.

'Fuck.' Kira gasped. Every technique she'd been taught, every coping mechanism burst into flame and crumbled into ash before she could reach for it. Two years. It had been two friggin' years since she'd been swamped. And this attack was a tsunami. Kira grasped at her throat, dug her nonexistent nails into her skin. 'I need to . . .'

Run. Get far away. Alone. Somewhere where no one else was taking her oxygen. Her T-shirt under her armpit was drenched. The stench of it filled her nostrils. Or maybe that was the cow shit. Hard to tell. Up was down and down was up right now. She ran. Pushed her feet through the quicksand. Stumbled down the hill, Vail's call ringing out behind her.

'Kira, focus on my voice. Please stop!'

Wizard he may be, but as a counsellor he needed more work. She couldn't focus. Her brain was stewed to mush under the flood of panic. Car. Get to it. Run. Never mind the lead in your legs. Just run from it. Jesus, was her heart pounding? Maybe it was malfunctioning. Shit. Shit. Shit. She was giving her unbreakable heart a heart attack. Going to die out here. Car. Get to it.

Door open. Body thrown into seat. Ignition started. Young boy in rearview mirror. Running after her. Mobile phone pressed to his ear. Other hand waving.

Pedal pressed. Vail became a tiny dot behind her. Her brain rattled in her skull as she ploughed the car through potholes. White knuckles. Actual, white knuckles. Roaring, straining engine. Very unhappy car. Sweat droplets forming on her chin, throat so tight her vision swum. Where was the fucking air? Grabbing the window lever, wrenching it hard.

'Oh shit.' Window lever in her metal hand. Not attached to the door. 'Fuck.' She slammed her arm against the window and glass shattered. Some of it rained into her lap. The twinkling, delicate sound exploded in her synapses, and all at once she was back there. In that crumpled wreck, flames licking at the hood that was wrapped around a hulking great tree trunk. Blood filled her throat. And the stench of flames and rubber suffocated her. A putrid, gut-wrenching scent. He was there. Beside her. And she knew the moment she looked at him that it was way too late for anything but grief. Her father's eyes were open, fixed on the tree ahead of them. The one she'd slammed them into. Kira sank into the pain, let it engulf her as she laid her head on the steering wheel and waited for the flames to take her, too.

The blast of an air horn roared through the shitbox. Kira lifted her head and cried out. The here-and-now was back. And coming in the form of a very unhappy semitrailer driver, currently bearing down on the blue piece of crap crawling across the road. She'd driven herself out onto the main road. Kira slammed her foot down on the accelerator, and the car lurched forward so hard her neck cracked. The truck swerved around her and continued on, driver blasting the horn a few more times as he went.

'Shit.' Too late Kira hit the brakes, and the car slid, nice and neat, into the ditch on the far side of the road. She scrambled out of her seat, fell onto hands and knees on the gravel, and threw up.

Tamas - 32

Tamas reclined in the wheelchair that had carried him from the medical ward to the Orientation Room. He regarded Captain Nex's holographic image with an inner smile. It was the only time the imposing Syranian was reduced to a height shorter than Tamas. Eron stood a few feet behind his captain, arms behind his back, his beautiful profile on display. His cheekbones had been carved by a master. He and the captain stood at a set of floor-to-ceiling windows looking out over a cityscape etched with a plethora of shimmering skyscrapers. High above the earth, while Tamas sat beneath it.

Blinking advertising signs added colour to the electric panorama. The city pulsed with life, the population enjoying the holiday and the perfect afternoon. Tamas had never been to New Weston, had never visited the executive penthouse he had paid for. Never wanted to. He hated cities with their impersonal air and frantic pace. People like him got trodden on in those places.

At least, people like the one he used to be. Tamas touched his fingers to the back of his hand and could actually feel the vibration of the utukku beneath the skin. They had not deserted him entirely when he'd transferred to Reuben. A shadow remained, ghosting through his veins. Warm as alcohol. Far more pleasant now than when they had ripped like hot coals through him to reach Blake.

'Any problems, Captain?'

'No significant issues to report.' Nex bit down on his words. 'We have some concerns about Eron's handling of Agar. The gallu is by far the strongest of the Four. I am keeping the initial recons limited to just a couple of hours. Any longer and I doubt Eron would be able to maintain a satisfactory level of control.' Captain Nex was not a forgiving alien. His disdain for his god-soldier was evident in the sneer of his lip, but Eron didn't flinch. 'Already he has reason to believe that Agar may be responsible for a death.'

It was far too early to be drawing the attention of the police. The gallu had been out on their leashes for just a few hours. 'Do the authorities suspect anything, Eron?'

In the past, speaking so directly, even to a hologram, would have seen Tamas break out in a sheen of sweat. His skin was dry to the touch.

'No, sir.' Eron met his gaze through the holographic haze. 'I was able to remove him from the location before there was any causal link. The human suffered a fall from a balcony along the parade route. Intoxication is being blamed, but Agar's aggression levels are substantial. Both physical, and sexual. And the effect on those he comes into contact with are intense and immediate. This has caused some issues for me in terms of keeping close to the gallu, as I advised the captain.'

Tamas lifted an eyebrow, impressed with the hard edge to Eron's words. Of all the Syranians, Eron had always been the most demure. Soft-spoken, eyes lowered more often than not. His fling with Kira had come utterly out of left-field. Tamas never doubted the sly bitch had manipulated the situation with all her usual flair. She was a cashed-up whore who thought she could take anything she wanted and pay nothing for it.

'Well done, Eron.' Tamas smiled at the Syranians, silently marvelling at his sudden ability to do so. No blush, no trembling. As though the utukku had eaten away that old version of himself. 'I trust you will rest now.'

Eron's gaze shifted to his captain. 'I'm awaiting instruction —'

'Rest.' As nice as they were to look at, Eron's cheeks were more sunken than Tamas remembered. The radiance had been released, so to a certain extent the hunt would take on a life of its own. 'You will rest. I'm sure that's what the captain would wish. Isn't that right, Nex?'

Tamas couldn't recall if he'd ever referred to the captain simply by his name. He had certainly never told the Syranians what to do so directly. At least, not without drowning beneath a flood of stuttered words. He knew the captain had doubted his ability to handle the goddess's Callings from the moment they'd met. Indeed, he'd been indignant from the get-go that humans need be involved at all. Nex was many things, but he was not good at holding a poker face.

Captain Nex's sharp nose lifted, but he nodded. A single jab of his chin. 'It seems prudent. Fatigue is dangerous. And we do not have time to spend chasing wayward gallu if they manage to escape the restraint of the mea stones. The carapaces will enable them to survive in this world for an untold length of time.'

'Forever, if I recall you correctly.'

'A considerable amount of time.'

'And that would not please the gods, now would it, Nex?' The flush of the utukku inside him must have been doing something to his senses; there was really no reason to waste time

antagonising the captain. Tamas had far better and greater things to
do. Still, to front up to the alien who'd had loomed over him for
the past few years was, quite frankly, exhilarating. And it distracted
him from what lay in the shrine just a short distance away.

'Indeed not. And I believe they are already displeased
enough with Azrael's disappearance, which I understand you are no
closer to resolving.' Captain Nex was no fool. He hadn't led armies
on his own world to be befuddled by a human man on this one.

'I've initiated various courses of action,' Tamas said, 'and
expect that the gallu's return will be imminent.'

He stopped short of revealing Azrael's true identity to the
captain, certain for reasons outside his understanding that the
goddess did not wish the identity to be known. From the moment
he awoke from their dreamscape encounter it had been fixed within
him. No one should know the gallu's identity. If he were not
entirely mistaken, and it was very possible he was, Tamas sensed a
certain embarrassment radiating from the goddess. A simmering
incredulity that Enkidu had escaped her.

'Very well, keep me informed.' The captain ended the
transmission.

Tamas was left staring at empty air. He sighed, leaning back
in the wheelchair, and tilted his head towards the shrine. He could
just make out the silhouette of Blake's body within the structure,
lying flat on the floor. The flowing Waters that moved down the
walls distorted her image. And just as she had remained when he'd

set the utukku on her, then again when he'd driven the goddess's blade into her wrist, Blake was infuriatingly silent. Not even a whimper throughout his conversation with Nex. Nor in the hour before that as Tamas sat in the greater Orientation Room.

Moving the chair to the base of the steps in the shrine, Tamas worked hard to not let a single gasp or grunt escape him as he hauled himself upright and made his way into the enclosure. He would not allow Blake the monopoly on fortitude. If she could stay quiet while the goddess inflicted her, he sure as hell wasn't about to whimper about a few flesh wounds. He was a Messenger. She was a traitor.

'Hello, Blake. How are you settling in?'

Blake lay at the base of the petrified trunk at the heart of the shrine. He had driven a piece of that trunk, a narrow sliver of wood,into her right wrist. Ereshkigal's 'blade', was little more than a splinter. But it was all the goddess required, a conduit through which she could inflict her punishment. Blake wore a Telteriun collar around her neck, and a short length of chain connected it to a spike embedded deep in the wood. She was curled up in a foetal position, facing him. Her eyes, bloodshot to a point where there was more red than white, fluttered open. Thin black lines veined the bare skin on her arms and beneath her collarbones where her blouse gaped. The top button had been torn free, probably in her surprisingly energetic display in the elevator. He knew Rossiter had given her some training in defence, but he'd never dreamed she was capable of rendering two guards almost senseless. Tamas made a mental note to locate the bodyguard. When he learned of Blake's incarceration, there would be issues.

'What do you want, Tamas?' Raspy and barely coherent, Blake's words still held bite.

He hesitated. There'd been no need to come here and set up the holoconnect in the Orientation Room to hold his conversation with Nex. There was indeed no need to have Blake remain in the Shrine at all. In time, he would have her relocated to a cell, but that time would be at *his* choosing. When he tired of the odd, comforting rush it gave him. To see Blake like this, laid low, suffering at the hand of a god she had so steadfastly denied. It caused the adrenaline to pulse through him in a way he'd not known before. And he was not ready to let it go.

Like the people who paid to see the Elephant Man, he wanted to be the one on the outside, relieved that it wasn't him. He needed to see what happened to someone who defied the gods.

It wasn't pretty. Her clothing was drenched with sweat, and the smell of it was heavy in the air. The bandage on her hand was brown with dried blood. And the dark rings under her eyes were so thick they looked painted on. But she raised herself onto one elbow, glaring at him.

'If you're here, then I'm guessing you haven't found what you're looking for.' She coughed and it set the chain tinkling, as though it were delicate and fine. Which it was not.

'But I will. You know that, I know that. And then –' He swept his hand towards her and then up towards the roof of the shrine were the totems kept baleful watch. 'Kira will share your fate. I know you two are not the best of friends, but blood is thick, so they say. But the guilt must burn you up. Knowing that your decision to take what was not yours, will kill your sister—'

'Get away from me!' Blake screamed. She rose up on her knees and launched herself at him. Tamas wasn't quick enough to suppress his own surprised gasp as he leapt out of her reach. Aside from the smallest twitch of fingers or blink of the eyes, any movement on Blake's part should have been impossible. The chain was intended for dramatic effect only, but it proved to be his saving grace. Its short length stopped her abruptly, the force of it toppling her backwards. Tamas pressed his hand to his belly. The utukku fluttered like a flock of sharp-clawed birds within him. Tamas spun around and raced as quickly as his wounded, tired body would allow out of the shrine.

'Touch her and I'll kill you, Tamas!' Blake screeched, voice cracking and lifting in all the wrong places. 'Do you hear me? I'll bring your whole bloody world down on top of you. I'll do it. And I won't care. I won't care!'

Her scream followed him as he moved down the stairs. Forgoing the wheelchair, he limped across the Orientation Room, head pounding beneath the bandages, desperate to be out of the room and far away from the madness and hate rushing after him. He stepped into the hallway.

'Close the door!' he shouted at the guards who waited for him there. Under strict instructions not to enter, it hadn't stopped them from hearing what had just gone on. And their confusion was written all over their faces.

'Sir, is everything all right?'

Tamas braced against the wall, swiping at the guard who tried to assist him. He didn't bother to answer a question that was none of their goddamn business. As his heart rate slowed and his breathing steadied, fury began to replace the panic. He'd just scampered out of there like a damn reticent child scolded by his mother. His insane mother. That look on Blake's face . . . Tamas closed his eyes and slammed his cast-bound wrist against the wall.

'Sir —'

'Fuck off.' The words exploded, ripe and raw and foreign. He barely swore under his breath, let alone at anyone around him.

'Sir, I apologise, but it's important.'

Tamas opened his eyes. An older man, smoke-grey hair and eyes to match, stood there.

'Sir, we've received word from Reuben —'

Finally.

'He's found them?'

'They detected a low-level radiance spike from a location a couple of hours' drive from Beleiro and are en route now. Reuben told us to inform you his…gut instinct…rates the likelihood it is Kira and the carapace as extreme.'

The man's jaw worked, clearly bemused by the odd message. If he knew Reuben at all, it was hardly surprising. The guard was ex-military, normally reliant on hard information and calculated plans. Not gut feelings. But it was the other piece of information that caught Tamas's attention.

'A radiance spike?' Tamas scowled at the ground, thoughts racing over one another. Reuben had been in Beleiro almost twelve hours, but the utukku detected no trace of Kira much beyond the hotel. She'd covered her tracks remarkably well. So why the sudden radiance spike? Tamas had never stopped to consider that Blake had smuggled a control cuff out with Kira and Azrael. He supposed it was possible Kira had in her possession one of the cuffs that could release the radiance, but considering she was trying to keep him hidden, it seemed counterintuitive to light him up like a Christmas tree. Perhaps she had had no choice? Maybe there was a malfunction? Either way, something significant had occurred with the gallu.

'Contact surveillance,' Tamas directed. 'Advise them to ready my remote-relay equipment. I'd like to be there when they reach the location.'

Kira - 33

Kira shivered against the breeze. Her top lip was damp, and her shirt clung to her boobs as though she were in a wet T-shirt competition. No way in all hells she was getting back in the car. Had no idea how she'd got into it in the first place. At least she'd found the oxygen in the air. Little bastard was right there all along. Just had to open her mouth and breathe. All it had taken to remind her was nearly getting mowed down by a semi. A panic attack like that hadn't rocked her world in years. But then, her world hadn't ever been like this. Ever.

She ran her fingers through her hair, making more of a mess of the already disastrous situation.

'Come on, you silly cow. Get up.' Kira followed her own advice and dragged herself to her feet. Tan Queen was going to be pissed about the broken window. Kira stifled a yawn, sucker-punched after the extreme high of the freak-out. Surely Vail would follow her. She couldn't have driven that far in her semi-psychotic state. Based on her memory, she thought the distance from the main road to the hill was walkable. Kid seemed fit. He'd turn up – any second now – and drive them back to the farm, 'cause Kira sure as hell wasn't getting behind the wheel. Vail might even confess to breaking the window. He was that type of kid. Too damn nice. She should take him shopping when all this was over.

A squawk disturbed the silence, coming from the tree line that stretched along the side of the road for as far as the eye could see. Which was only really up to the next corner where the asphalt curved out of sight. The squeaking monster in the bushes was a bird, probably. She was no zoologist, but it needed to shut the fuck up. It was making her head ache. More. Kira gave up fighting the urge to lie down. The hood was warm under the sun and fucking uncomfortable against the nubs of her spine, but it would do. Sky as blue as the Mediterranean. Kira thumped her fist against the hood. *Great comparison, K.* Her thoughts now raced down the Nina pathway.

Kira the easy target. Ouch.

She rolled her head from side to side, hoping that might dislodge everything. A speck in the sky off to the north caught her eye. Just above the trees. She sat up and squinted, shading her eyes. It was hard to tell if the thing was super far away or just small. It hugged the trees, shifting from the north to the south, drawing closer. Might be a helicopter? Two-seater kind? The craft drew steadily closer, so low to the trees she half expected it to drop down beneath the canopy. It didn't. It moved out over the road, coming into full view.

Square in shape, four propellers at each corner, hugging a metal framework that in turn encased a solid black box. Not a helicopter. Not even close. One tenth the size.

Drone.

'You are kidding me,' Kira said. 'You are fucking kidding me.'

She shoved herself off the hood, legs threatening to buckle at the sudden movement, and crouched behind the car. The Facility used drones for security the way Kira used pot to relax. They manufactured some, too. Drones, not Mary Jane.

Kira knew that 'cause Perry was always bugged her about getting one for him. Every birthday he'd pretend to be bummed when one didn't show up. Kira wiped her hand across her damp face. She very seriously doubted this drone belonged to some farmer checking on his cows.

The craft rose up over the trees on the opposite side of the road, moving further away. It dipped down low before rising back up again, and moving like a metallic vulture around something on the ground. Something like a gobsmacked kid with a bad haircut.

'Vail, goddamn it.' She knelt beside the open driver's door, flexing and unflexing her fists. Get in, goddamn it. Get the kid out of there. If she had anything left to puke, she'd be puking it right now at the thought of driving. Whoa. Hold horses. Tamas didn't know Vail from a bar of soap. And she had to assume it was Tamas's little pet up in the sky. Even if they spotted Vail, they'd have no reason to home in on him. They were looking for her. And they were sphincter-clenchingly close.

Think like a fugitive, Kira. Think.

A decent fugitive would have driven off by now. She was not a decent fugitive. Kira did get in the car, but only to search it on the off-chance that there was something useful in there. Like a phone. She should call the big guy to come manhandle her out of this shit. Kira flung open the glovebox.

Handgun. *Leona, you spicy little minx.* Witches be packing. But no phone. Not even a bag of snacks. The low buzz of an engine reached her. Kira tried to back out of the car, catching her shirt on the gearstick and telling it exactly what she thought of it. Which was very little.

'Oh for fuck's sake.'

Two forest-green Hummers hurtled down the road towards her. Subtle as a fucking brick. One of them swung right, taking the dirt road where she'd left Vail. The other made a beeline straight for her.

Shit.

One of the rear doors slid open. She had time to *think* about running, but none left over to actually do the act. Two chunks of metal propelled themselves from the vehicle. Grimalkin. Her day just got a whole tonne worse. The robotic absurdities were her very least favourite thing to ever come out of the Facility R&D Department. Sleek, black, headless mechanical big cats. Three of them loped towards her. Who in their right mind designed something that looked and moved like a panther, but didn't put a head on the thing? The cats were damn freaky. And worse, they were forcing her hand. She had to get back in the car.

Kira scrambled like a manic spider into the driver's seat, hand shaking before it even touched the wheel. The grimalkin were barely ten metres away. Unlike her arm, their titanium metal did gleam in the light. Whoever was in the Hummer didn't seem too bothered about her getting away. Smug pricks pulled up a couple of metres away. Just sat there. Watching. Best give them a show then.

Shitbox didn't let her down, despite what she'd done to it. Started first go. Shifting into reverse, Kira turned to look over her shoulder. Like a pack of circling hyenas, the grimalkin had all sides covered. In movement they were big cat, but in height they were Great Dane. Their shoulders were level with Kira's line of sight.

'Here goes really bad idea number ten thousand.' Kira pressed hard on the accelerator, unsteady stomach loathing every second of movement. The car jerked, once, twice and then hurtled out of the ditch. Rust-pocked beast had some go in it, she'd give it that much. But it wasn't going to like what she wanted to do with it. Kira aimed for the grimalkin skulking right behind her. The mech-cat had no eyelids to bat, and no programming to instruct it to flinch. So it did neither. The crunch of metal on metal triggered a shit-load of bad, bad memories, and the impact stopped the car dead. Kira's ribs slammed into the bottom of the steering wheel, her older Azrael-inflicted bruise saying hello with sharp teeth. But the grimalkin went down.

And got straight back up again.

Not a scratch or a dent on its slimline body. She might as well have rammed a brick wall. Pressing fingertips gingerly to her ribcage, Kira decided she could cross this idea off the list. She grabbed the handgun.

'And now, really bad idea number ten thousand and one.'

She jumped out of the car, leaving the motor running. 'Fuck off, asshole!' she shouted at the Hummer and its shadowy occupants. It was very, very tempting to say, *You'll never take me alive*, but pissing on fate would be shit idea number ten thousand and two. The grimalkin kept their distance, standing completely still –

as unnerving as when they moved. The doors of the Hummer opened. Kira jabbed the gun towards the vehicle. 'Not kidding. I'll use this.'

A man and a woman—clad in the standard Facility ensemble; all black material with patches on the shoulders that held the faintest sheen—stepped out each side of the Hummer, their own weapons – bigger of course – trained on her. 'I do not believe you will.' The woman's voice was like a GPS, calm and smooth and irritating. Her blonde curls were ridiculously voluminous and perky, and her snot 'Kira, make this easy on yourself and put down the gun.'

The man moved closer. A smug grin creased his pudgy olive-skinned face. 'You're done, Kira. And you just made our day. Main team is headed further east looking for you. Man, were you ever in the wrong place at the wrong time.'

Kira edged in behind the open car door.

'They come back to you yet, Dillon?' Miss GPS asked. 'Where do we take our prize?'

'Nothing yet. Probably pissed we won this one.'

Dillon reminded Kira of a cabana boy she'd met in Spain, few years back. So full of himself she was surprised he didn't choke on it. Why did neither of them give a shit she had a gun? She could use it. One lesson, two years ago, counted. *Fuck, at least act worried.*

'Kira, lower the weapon. Don't waste our time.'

Oh screw you, pool boy. Kira took aim at a space over the Hummer and pulled the trigger. Nothing. Not a peep.

'Idiot,' Kira hissed and pulled back the safety catch.

She fired again and the rebound caught her off guard, slamming her elbows into her ribs. 'Mother-goddamn-fucker.'

The grimalkin to her right was first to move, lowering its body, stalking in towards her exactly like a lion approaching its prey. It was far more graceful than a bunch of nuts and bolts were allowed to be. Kira levelled the gun towards it, hesitating. Chances were the thing was bulletproof. She might end up with a ricochet piercing her brain. Hell of a way to go. And her hesitation was all the headless piece of shit needed. In one fluid move it rushed in towards her, lifted a front leg, and with a precisely aimed blow kicked the gun clean from her hands. Kira threw herself to one side but only managed to overbalance on the uneven ground. Down on hands and knees she went. In a quicksilver decision, she headed back into the ditch. Because getting to the trees and hiding in there, was *totally* do-able. Bad idea number –

A whispery sound filled the air, and something gripped her ankle before she was yanked backwards. The momentum shoved her onto her belly, and she was dragged back up the slight incline.

'Get the hell off me.' She kicked out with her free leg, flipping over onto her back. Gravel went all kinds of uninvited places as the grimalkin's restraint pulled her towards the asphalt. They had her lassoed like a damn steer at a rodeo. Kira grabbed the edge of the car door, clinging to it like a toilet bowl at three a.m. 'Let me go, you assholes.'

But the couple hadn't moved any closer. Dillon and the woman, a curly-haired piece of shit that Kira would deal with later, just watched. The grimalkin she'd tried to mow down with the car stepped up. Tentacles, goddamn tentacles, rushed out of the panel where a head should be. She pressed against the side of the car but only succeeded in making things easier for the mech-monster. One long, slithering line gripped her left arm, the other circled the armadillo, pinning her to the side of the car. She bucked her hips and twisted her shoulders but quickly decided that would only end up hurting her and getting her nowhere. The grimalkin was so close she could smell the tang of metal and something else. Oil, perhaps.

'Oh, this is so not good.'

Finally, the man and woman approached, walking in that pacey way military types did. Both had secondary guns strapped to their thighs and grim determination plastered to their faces. What she wouldn't have given for that massive semi to reappear and take them both out. Actually, a strong vodka lime would have been even better. She winced. The pinch of the wire around her flesh arm was starting to bite.

Dillon stood beside the grimalkin. 'Let's keep this civil, Kira. Try to behave yourself. I'd like you to get to your feet now.'

'I'd like you to fuck off. Guess we can't all get what we want.'

How the hell had these shits found her?

'Yes, actually, we can,' the woman said. Some hint of an accent there. Russian maybe. Still totally GPS-like. 'Where is the property you removed from the Facility, Kira?'

Her hand grew numb, pins and needles trickling down the length of her arm. 'Oh sorry, was that *your* dildo I took? My bad. Only used it a few times. It's in the car if you'll let me get it.'

The slap to the face was unexpected. Stars bloomed in her vision.

'Answer the question, you self-entitled little –'

'Alexeev, take it easy,' Dillon said. 'Reuben said we need her in one piece.'

Reuben. Son. Of. A. Bitch. And the only idiot who seemed to find Tamas remotely interesting.

'Where is the carapace, Kira?' Alexeev's glare said she'd shifted into bad-cop mode, and had no intention of taking it easy. Her balled-up fist hovered way too close.

'Keep that up and you're going to turn me on.' Kira smiled, and winked. Her reward was a solid hit to the jaw. Teeth clacking hard. 'Fuck, what is your problem, asshat?'

But asshat turned to Dillon. 'Get her in the car.' She pulled her radio comms from its shoulder strap. 'Moore, do you copy?'

Static said Moore did not. 'Moore, we have Kira Beckworth but there's no sign of the carapace. What is the directive?'

A heap more static, apparently. Then just a couple of words, mangled up like spaghetti.

'Kid . . . get him . . . talk.'

Oh hell no. Not Vail.

'Don't touch him. Don't you fucking touch him!' Kira screamed. And damn it felt good. Heat flooded through her, blazed a trail right through the metal of her arm. She jerked forward, pushing all her body weight against the tentacles pinning her down. To her surprise her right shoulder broke free. Her momentum propelled her forward and she lashed out, not sure where she was aiming. Her clenched fist hit the solid trunk of Dillon's leg, right at the knee joint. There was a crack, like a giant ice cube hitting warm air, and the guy roared, falling to his side, hands gripping at his knee.

'Don't move.' Alexeev trained her gun on Kira. 'Stay down.' She grabbed at the comms. 'Arc Team requesting immediate assistance. Reuben, do you copy?'

A pitched squeal came from the device, loud enough to cause Alexeev to cry out. And unless Reuben had started to speak in Screech-ese, he did not copy at all.

The heat in the metal radiated up into Kira's shoulder and filled the right side of her chest. She grabbed hold of the tentacle wrapped around her flesh arm and wrenched it. The grimalkin propelled forward, headless-head-butting the car. Before her brain registered what her hands were doing, Kira rocked onto her knees, grabbed hold of the grimalkin's legs and flung the whole thing back towards Alexeev. The mech-cat had to be at least one hundred kilos of metal and wiring. It sailed through the air, headed right for the woman who stood staring open-mouthed at the projectile. Miss GPS was nothing if not agile. She threw herself out of the way, drop-rolled, and got back to her feet.

'Kira, back down or I will shoot!' she shouted.

'Put your hands in the air.' Dillon might be down for the count, but it hadn't stopped him from grabbing his own gun from its holster and levelling it at her. 'I will shoot you.'

No doubt there. And chances of avoiding it, next to nil. Tentacle-cat number two stepped up, ready to replace his far-flung buddy. The firey heat in her arm was fading. Her guts felt hollow as a vacuum. Kira slumped against the car.

'To your six, to your six.' Alexeev's voice cracked and her gun lifted.

Dillon quickly followed suit, pointing at something overhead. A thud rumbled through the car, vibrating against Kira's back. But she didn't look up. Didn't need to. The shadow spilling across the road in front of her told her plenty. The angel was back.

Eron - 34

The thumping in Eron's head finally reduced from the
sharpness of a knife blow to a dull ache. His body trembled with
spent energy, and his throat was rasped dry, but Eron held his head
high, shoulders back. Agar may sense the discomfort he was
imparting on his handler, but Eron refused to let it show
outwardly. There had been next to no opportunity for rest, despite
Tamas's instruction. Eron had had barely an hour's respite before
the captain had demanded he ready himself to depart.

Agar had refused to settle in his chamber, and unwilling to take the chance it wasn't just sheer boredom that drove the gallu, the captain had ordered them out. The chance that the radiance had already ebbed through enough of the population to locate Dumuzi seemed infinitesimal. The reassignment was ill-considered in Eron's mind, but he was hardly going to challenge Captain Nex.

Through a series of telepathic shoves and wrenches, Agar had guided Eron here, a small private hospital about a fifteen-minute journey from the penthouse. And Eron's suspicions that Agar toyed with him grew more fortified. The captain and Tamas had warned that, much the way a dog might seek out mud puddles, the Four found inordinate pleasure in pestilence. They hungered for the stench of disease. Now, pacing down the bleach-scented halls of the hospital, Eron suspected Agar had fooled him.

He hauled back on the Bind as Agar leered at a petite woman trying to pass them. Agar pushed his lips into what might pass for a smile, but the vapidness of the look was unsettling, and garnering more attention than was necessary. The nurse fairly crawled up the wall to avoid being any closer to the broad-shouldered baring down on her. Sweat beaded on Eron's forehead; the effort of holding Agar in check was no small thing. Least of all on so little sleep. And this choice of location puzzled him. It was a venue for the ill, there was death here. Dumuzi would be neither ill, nor dead.

Eron's hold on the Bind succeeded in slowing Agar's pace. 'Conceal yourself more effectively, or I will end this now.'

Agar levelled him with a glare that sought to strip the skin from his bones, and Eron's mind exploded in a spray of sharp needlepoints, jagged tips that formed into words.

And how do you intend to do that, little servant? Do not bore me with empty words.

Eron staggered, bracing himself against the wall, mouth pressed closed for fear of crying out. A few curious glances were thrown his way, but he was fortunate. Being unwell in a hospital corridor was hardly unreasonable. Catching his stolen breath, Eron forced himself to meet Agar's stare. Bel had spoken to him of this. A warning that, depending on the capabilities of the gallu, coherent telepathic communication may take place. But until now Agar's silence had been deep and ongoing. The gallu's amusement didn't reflect on his face, but it was there for Eron to sense. And it ignited a quiet rage. Eron grabbed Agar's arm; a solid construct of Syrana's precious Telteriun. The only metal in the known worlds capable of containing the immense power that was the Four.

Eron dug his fingers into the bulge of flesh at Agar's bicep. The carapace's outer body contained no pain receptors, but it gave Eron satisfaction to see his grip produce dents in the faux skin. 'Focus on the task at hand. You are here for Dumuzi, and nothing more. You'd do well to remember that. Move on.'

With the mea stone seeming to bore down deeper into his bone, Eron forced Agar on down the hallway. The gallu did not speak again, but cast a look at Eron that spoke of more unpleasantness to come.

Some of the humans milling about sent stares their way. A trio – two men and a woman – sat behind a desk, eyeing them but saying nothing. Agar increased his pace. Eron caught the faint echo of laughter following them down the hall, nervous excitement trembling through the sound. What an unsettling pair they must appear. Eron accepted some suggestions from Clara with his dress, pinning his hair back in a tight ponytail and hiding it beneath a faded forest-green beanie. A too-large brown suede jacket with sheepskin around the collar covered his slender arms and narrow shoulders; black trousers, chequered with a surprising array of utility pockets, covered his legs. The boots he wore were a little small and quite weighty, reaching up to midcalf. A masculine look, Clara advised, and the layers might go some way to covering the softer feminine curve of his hips, waist and buttocks. Not that she minded at all. Her words, uttered while finding a multitude of reasons to touch those very features.

Agar strode with purpose down the corridors. A right turn here, a left there. Clearly he had picked up the trace of something strong. Something holding all his attention now. He'd not so much as tried to toy with the Bind in all of five minutes. Five minutes of blissful reprieve for Eron. They reached a section where another reception desk sat to the right of the hall. Above the doorway a sign declared 'Intensive Care Unit'. Agar glanced at him, giving him a barely perceptible nod.

Here. There is trace here.

Eron pressed a hand to his chest, the telepathy's ferocity akin to being shouted at from an intimate distance. A young nurse, a generously weighted woman with blotchy skin and straw-like hair, stared at them, unblinking.

'Can I help you?'

Agar leaned on the desk, his gaze shifting up and down the nurse with an intimacy she seemed surprisingly unperturbed by.

'I hope so,' Eron said. 'My cousin has been brought into the unit. I was hoping to be able to see him.'

The girl's gaze swept over his body, taking in the differences he knew she saw there, despite the clothing masquerade.

'You can't go into the unit, I'm afraid,' she said.

Agar leaned over the low counter, and Eron scrambled to catch him, fearing his motive.

Leave me.

The stabbing thought made Eron recoil. And it gave Agar the moment he needed to grasp the girl's hand. She resisted for the briefest of seconds, then was still, eyes locked on Agar. The gallu said nothing. Nothing outward at least, and he let go of her before she had taken two full breaths. Her eyes grew unfocused, fixed on something at the desk before her. She pressed a black button to her right, and the doors of the ward swung open. The phone at her desk rang, and she picked up the call, vague nothingness still filling her expression. Eron and Agar filed into the ward, and her conversation continued with the caller as though nothing untoward at all had just happened.

Utter control with one simple touch.

Eron ran his hand over the mea stone on his forearm. This simple piece of rock protected him from becoming just as the human had been. Vulnerable. Controlled. At times it felt a dreadfully inadequate barrier.

The intensive care unit was small, an six-bed facility, but all the beds held a body, each with their own collection of beeping monitoring machines connected to each patient by a variety of wires. Desperately unwell humans, which meant none were Dumuzi himself, but presumably someone in this room had been in close proximity to the immortal. Agar stood just inside the door, body still, head tilted, as though testing the air for a scent. Two nurses, a man and a woman, tended to a patient at the far end of the ward. The woman looked up. Eron's pulses stirred to a faster pace. Her name flew into his mind before he could even think to check himself.

Kira.

But of course, it was not her. Aside from her chronic aversion to anything remotely associated with hospitals, Kira would simply never have spent so much time braiding her hair in the impressive way this woman had. She was older, too, on second glance. He had been most mistaken. Fatigued mind deceiving him, he supposed. Eron glanced at Agar, but the gallu gave no indication that he'd sensed any of Eron's fleeting thoughts. Eron walked away from him, meeting the woman halfway up the ward. He would need Agar to wipe the woman's memories of their presence, but for now he needed breathing space. A chance to push Kira back down into the deep, closed corner of his mind where he had thought her locked away. But Agar gave him no such chance, following close behind and taking the woman's hand as a gasp crossed her lips.

'What seems to be the problem with these people?' Agar's manufactured voice surprised Eron. Far softer and more pleasant than expected. Nothing like Agar's inner voice, scraped from the bottom of a dark and raw pit.

'They are displaying similar symptoms.' The familiar vacant look filled the woman's eyes. 'Fever and vomiting, a rash on their lower backs. No one has been prepared to name it, and it's unclear if it's a virus or a bacterial infection.'

'Oh, it's neither of those.' Agar smiled, too wide, and revealing far too many teeth. If the woman hadn't been in the grip of his hypnosis, Eron was sure she would have run from him screaming. 'You need to be somewhere else, both of you. Anywhere but here.'

The woman nodded, just a slight dip of her head, and called out to her colleague. They left the room without another word, moving with great purpose, as though they couldn't get to their destination fast enough.

'What is your interest here?' Eron pointed to the nearest bed, where a gaunt man with a disarming amount of facial hair lay. 'Who bares the trace of the demigod?'

Agar's sideways glance was definitively serpentine. *Patience.*

Eron afforded himself some congratulations for neither flinching nor so much as blinking when the word jackhammered through his skull. Agar sauntered his imposing frame to the bedside, moving as though he had not a care in the world. Eron uttered a silent prayer to Lahar, beseeching his god's good grace here. Foolish, Eron knew. To wish that this could be over so quickly, that they might locate Dumuzi so soon after the release of the Four, but the unease that came with being in Agar's presence grew with each moment.

Agar traced a finger along the bedcovers, from the bulge of the man's stomach all the way up the side of his neck. He splayed his fingers over the man's face, holding his palm just a centimetre above the tip of the nose. The skin on Agar's hand brightened as though lit from within, and tiny fissures opened in the lines of his palm. The man jolted, his belly lurching towards the ceiling, and fell back heavily against the mattress. The monitor he was attached to skipped a beep, stuttering like a bird that's suddenly forgotten its song, only to restart immediately in a slow, monotonous rhythm.

No.

Moving on, Agar performed the procedure on the man in the next bed, a young boy, surely no more than a teenager judging by the smattering of acne on his chin. Again nothing. They passed by the third bed. It held a woman. Dumuzi was reborn each time in male form. The gods and the power that enabled them had an odd fondness for rules and protocols. Even when binding a soul for an eternity here on Earth. The demigod had been originally imprisoned in a male body, and so it would remain.

Agar ignored several of the beds, his displeasure growing with each telepathic *No*. The thought spiked Eron's psyche, touching every nerve ending with a dull electricity. Finally, Agar stood with his hand over an elderly man. The dark-skinned man was hollow-cheeked with wiry white eyebrows. A plethora of tubes and wires fed into his body. Eron frowned. Dumuzi would not succumb to the radiance, so he would not grow so ill. Was Agar simply toying with these people? With Eron himself?

Agar's expression flickered, lines forming around his eyes as he narrowed them. He pressed both hands down upon the man's chest. The machine beside the bed erupted with a high screech of distress, and the man's eyes flew open. A second later, his eyeballs liquefied and gushed down his cheeks in a flood of thick tears.

'No!' Eron cried, throwing all his mental weight behind the Bind. The daggers returned in his skull as he fought to gain control over Agar. The gallu stepped away from the dead man and paced to the centre of the room, raising his hands high. He turned to look at Eron, his expression so blank he truly looked like a statue. A cold, hard piece of stone. A vein in Eron's forehead pulsed.

Come, Eron, you might see that there is some pleasure to be found in their pain. Open to me.

Agar's force shuddered against him, a singular, solid wave of power that threatened to engulf Eron whole. A raw . . . beautiful . . . mesmerising energy. He forced a breath into his pressured chest. There would be such ease in letting go. The wave beckoned him. Inviting. Promising an end to discomfort.

Agar pointed a finger towards the young boy. Just the barest flick of his finger and the boy's body contorted, hands clawing at the mattress beneath him. Agar intended to destroy them all.

Eron raged against himself, pummelling back Agar's mindful power of suggestion. If Eron lost control of the gallu, the creature would abandon the task of finding Dumuzi as easily as he had just crushed the old man's mind.

Focusing in tightly on the Bind, Eron threw a solid wall of power at Agar. The gallu let out a cry, too high for any of the humans to have heard, but it rent through Eron's eardrums. He held fast, choking off Agar's energy, pulling it in tight and nailing it down hard against the Bind. When Eron turned and walked out of the ward, Agar followed, like a scolded but unrepentant child. They walked out of the hospital and into the dullness of evening, not a word passing between them. They stepped into the waiting vehicle before the doctors and nurses roused from their stupors. All the way back through the city, the memory of the touch of Agar's raw power sat like an unpleasant secret at the back of Eron's mind. It followed him as they returned to the penthouse, and was undiminished even by the time he hauled Agar into the containment chamber and bound him in his glass prison. Eron released far more inhibitor than was necessary, watching Agar's body drop like a stone to the concrete floor. But any satisfaction was eroded by Agar's ever-present smirk. That twist of his lips that had not left his face since the hospital.

Eron seated himself on the couch closest to the window, where he had an uninterrupted view of a city slowly dipping into evening. Shadows from the skyscrapers reached out across the streets. Alone in the penthouse, he sighed, resting his head back against the soft leather. Every joint ached, every fibre tense and stretched to its limit, his forearm heavy with the weight of the stone; now a dead weight making every movement difficult. All that remained was the heat of Agar's ecstasy. Inflicting such easy death had placed the gallu on a high, the likes of which Eron fought to push from his mind even now.

'Good afternoon.' Clara's soft voice filled the air, her white-toothed smile firmly in place. She wore a short white skirt and a bright orange blouse which clung to the subtle swell of her breasts. No bra, nipples pushing at the fine fabric. 'Can I get you anything?'

'If I were in need of something, I would have asked you for it.' His reply was curt and disdainful, but it did not even seem to register with Clara. She dipped her head, subduing her ever-ready smile into a serious line.

'Of course. If you change your mind, I am at your disposal —'

'I'm well aware of that. Thank you,' Eron said. 'I'd appreciate being left alone for a moment. Is the captain here?'

'No. Captain Nex has gone out to work alongside Bel for a short while. If you require food, it is available in the dining room.'

Her saccharine smile made irritation boil through him. And the way she bit her lip, the gentle thrust forward of her hips, made his empty stomach turn. The woman's subservience was pathetic, and despite what she might have heard, he would not debase himself so easily. Eron stalked away, unzipping the bulky jacket, pulling it from his shoulders, desperate to feel the weight of it gone. All he wanted now was a long, hot shower. New missions were planned for tonight, as humans congregated in clubs and bars and cinemas, to released the radiance further into the population. Another evening spent fighting Agar's tremendous weight.

Eron caught the odour of food and detoured into the dining room. The glass table at the room's centre held a pizza box. Eron's true earthly love. He grabbed a slice, suddenly ravenous. The large plasma-screen TV was on. With the slice halfway to his mouth, Eron froze. Riots had broken out in the northeast of the city, looting and assaults. The authorities were still trying to work out what had triggered the violence, with the police struggling to keep it all under control. No one had died yet, but in the north ten people had been taken to the hospital with serious injuries, and many local shops were on fire. The camera panned to take in a wide view, and Eron saw the hulking outline of the sports stadium he had gone to with Agar the night before.

'Clara,' Eron called.

She reappeared with astonishing brevity.

'Eron? Can I help you?' The way she said his name, with a breathless familiarity, stirred the same wave of irritation that had seen him banish her just a few minutes ago. But he needed to know.

'These riots,' he gestured to the TV, 'was Bel with Diresh in those northeast suburbs last night?'

She brushed a strand of her hair behind her ears. 'Yes. He was. It appears there is reason to believe the gallus' presence has a side effect. Unfortunate, I suppose.' She stood so close her perfume filled Eron's nostrils. 'It seems the gallus trigger heightened levels of aggression in many human contacts.'

'The captain is aware of this?'

'Yes.'

'He said nothing to me.'

For the first time, Clare appeared unsure of herself, brushing at her immaculately pressed blouse. 'I'm sorry. I'm not sure why.'

But he knew exactly why. The captain still doubted Eron's conviction. His ability to remain detached when the humans began to tear each other apart.

Eron threw his slice of pizza back into the box, his appetite vanished.

Kira - 35

Azrael's wings arched from his back, throwing a shadow over Kira. Considering the circumstances, her first thought was ludicrous, but fuck the guy was absolutely jaw-droppingly beautiful, like some kind of ethereal Levi's jeans commercial photoshopped to within an inch of its life. The wings didn't just make him physically wider; it was more than that. He was billboard epic.

But Az only had eyes for the guns pointed at him.

'Stand down.' Now Alexeev found her cool. Gun nozzle steady as it fixed on Az. 'Stand down.'

Just beyond the hired-heavy lay the grimalkin Kira had slam-dunked. She'd not only managed to hurl it to the other side of the road, but she'd also damn well killed the thing. A dull ache hummed at her collarbone. Her fingertips searched it out – and brushed metal.

'What the fuck?' Kira hissed, tilting her head, trying to peer down at herself. The armadillo had spread, covering the right side of her neck. 'Jesus christ.' Kira pressed at her chest. More metal. Reaching almost to her boob. Seriously? Metal tits? Fuck no. And thank fuck she hadn't bothered to re-bra after her sessions with Caleb.

'I said don't move!' Alexeev shouted.

'Piss off.' Couldn't the dickhead see her personal crisis here? Her prosthetic was trying to eat her. 'You didn't say don't move you said—'

'Shut the hell up, Kira. Just shut your pathetic mouth.' Dillon knelt on his good knee, the other leg propped at an awkward angle. The gun in his hands shook, his lips the grey-green shade of rotten meat. He looked like shit, but the only thing Kira felt bad about was that she hadn't dislocated his other kneecap.

'Do not move.' Alexeev's voice was like her grip. Impressively steady. 'Do not move, or I will fire.'

A soft beeping sound came from the comms device attached to her shoulder. The two surviving grimalkin stood beside her. Stock-still, like super-elaborate garden statues. As it turns out, Az was in no mood for following orders. The shadow lifted from Kira as Az's wings drew up into the air. And the grimalkin went ballistic. Their faceless front panels glowed white.

'Oh shit,' Kira cried. A blast of white light exploded from each of the mech-cats. Death by headless cat. Never saw that one coming. The whole soggy mess she called a life was done again. This time for reals. The grimalkin's firepower thundered around her, loud enough to wake the dead in every nearby universe. She probably should have been more terrified, more desperate to survive. Should have opened her eyes at least. But really, she'd been numb for years. Since the accident. Just didn't have the care factor. Stick a fork in her. Just let her be done.

Kira cowered behind her raised arms. Any second now.

But she didn't die.

Again.

Fuck.

She blinked against a kaleidoscope of specks. Az crouched in front of her. The bulk of his wings extended out to shield her, but the tips folded back in front of him, two miniature shields for his own body. She peered out from between his legs. The two grimalkin were prepping for another go. White light darted around the rectangular shape of their no-heads. Round and round the perimeter, growing brighter with each circuit. Then boom. The world exploded again. Kira shielded her face, determined to get a look at what the hell was going on. Whatever those mech-cats were spewing at Az, it wasn't doing what was intended. And then, something new to add to Az's bag of tricks. A halo formed around his body, the light reflecting off the metal of his wings in shimmering waves, as if caught in some kind of gravity there.

He sliced his wings forward, moving so quickly they were no more than a silver streak through the air. The moment he began to move, a rush of heat shot through Kira's chest. She glanced down, half-expecting to see her clothes smouldering. Nothing. Azrael lunged forward, and with a move that would have looked legit in a ballet, he sliced through one of the grimalkin. The mech-cat might as well have been made from butter, falling open in two neat halves. A multitude of wires in its guts instantly soldered. Shots rang out. No sign of calm now from former Miss GPS.

'Don't destroy the target!' she screamed.

Dillon didn't give a fuck apparently, firing off round after round. Az the not-so-human shield was doing a stellar job, somehow managing to deflect the close-proximity onslaught, but it was getting too ridiculously close for comfort.

Kira staggered to her feet, cowering in behind Az. Light, bright red this time, spewed into the air and a killer Fourth of July display sparked against Az's shoulder, sending him lurching backwards.

'Oh fuck.' Kira dove out of his way, body-slamming herself against the pavement, the stones burying themselves in all the wrong places. A narrow red laser tried to follow Az's evasive path but instead burned a neat horizontal line through the body of the shitbox. With Az standing over her, Kira dragged herself along the ground, the thick scent of smouldering metal scorching the air. The armadillo was toasty. Way too toasty. As if it were sucking up all the heat being thrown at them.

Az's wings darted up and down, transformed into guillotines as he fended off both bullets and lasers. The attacks pinged off the metal like ping-pong balls. Kira scrambled along the length of the car on all fours. A bullet thudded into the front wheel of the car a second before she reached it, air hissing from the tyre as she cursed and swore her way past. A spray of glass showered down on her, the front window shattering under the touch of the mech-cats' laser load. Fuck, Leona was going to be so, so pissed about her car.

An ear-piercing scream froze Kira to the spot. The armadillo's heat ratcheted up a notch, as if she were holding it over a fire. She darted a glance back. Wished she hadn't. Alexeev was on her knees. It was the start of a very bad day for her. Blood poured from a gash that stretched from one side of her torso to the other. She pressed her hands to her stomach, as though that might stem the torrent of red leaving her. It didn't. Not even close. Alexeev's eyes rolled back in her head, and she went down face first into a sea of red.

Azrael turned, and the remains of Kira's lunch threatened to projectile. 'Christ.'

Blades forming the tip of Az's left wing were dark with blood. And something else. A chunk of something you should only find in a butcher's shop. Az had his other hand knuckle-deep in the face panel of one of the grimalkin, now a bowling ball with legs.

Kira fast-tracked it on hands and knees, not giving a shit about the gravel anymore, survival instinct back with a vengeance. Way too many cause of death options here. And ending up as a chunk on the tip of Az's wings wasn't way up there on her list of must-haves. She leaned against the radiator, breathing like a chick in labour. Short and sharp.

Don't think about the meat chunk. Don't think about the meat chunk.

She pressed her metal hand to her belly, flesh hand overlaying it. The metal was cool to the touch. Not remotely warm. But the feedback coming from the sensors said warm, warm, warm. Seriously, what was going on with the armadillo? The thing had gone fucking bat-shit. Her world was malfunctioning. And Az wasn't done yet.

Still clutching the grimalkin, he strode towards Dillon, the metal corpse making a god-awful screech against the surface of the road. Kira clasped her hands to her ears, trying to deaden down the madness. Dillon, the poor son-of-a-bitch, was making the world's worst attempt to get away – on his back, scrambling backwards like a deranged crab. If he hadn't shit his pants yet, it was coming real soon.

'Stand down,' he shouted. 'Stand down. I've radioed it in. You will need to surrender.'

Kira stifled a laugh. A panicked, freaked-out, slightly insane laugh. Surrender? The dude was kidding, right?

Dillon's eyes couldn't have gotten any wider if he'd had someone peeling back his eyelids. He flipped onto his front, trying to high-tail it on all fours. Azrael straddled him. He grabbed the terrified man by his hair, pulling his head back at an angle that made Kira cringe. She clung to the headlight, still not certain she wouldn't hurl. The sense of warmth in her arm began fading. Sensors readjusting maybe. Azrael's wings shifted about him, bobbing with the movement of his body. Blood ran from where the wings protruded from his back. His shirt was torn to shreds by the metal. *Fucking impressive, Blake. Sickening, but impressive.*

Azrael placed one foot squarely in the middle of Dillon's back. The man hissed something from between clenched teeth, one arm straining to reach back and land a blow on Azrael's leg. Azrael wrenched him so his back curved in an arch. Kira dug her fingertips into the rim of the headlight. That guy she'd babysat in the glass cells at the Facility, the one who had no clue how to drink a beer, had well and truly left the building. And the new Az was kind of a scary motherfucker.

'What do you want from me?' Spittle flew from Dillon's mouth, his voice strained.

Az didn't hesitate. 'It is you who seem to want something from me.'

'Go back to hell.' Dillon, the cabana boy, twisted like a fish fresh-pulled from the water. At this rate he'd break his own neck.

Azrael lowered himself onto one knee. His wings moved in towards his spine, giving Kira a clear view of the impromptu interrogation session. Considering Dillon was an asshole and had just tried to kill her, Kira should have been less empathetic. But scary Az was, well, scary as all hell. As though he could reach down and tear the Earth open if he got shitty enough. It was actually kind of hot. But she could think that 'cause she was on his good side. His very good side. Chances were he wasn't going to gut her, not on purpose. Chances were not so great for this poor fuck.

Az leaned down, putting his mouth close to Dillon's ear. Kira pulled herself to her feet, still hugging the car like it was a tin comfort blanket.

'I have been there. And I will not return.' Azrael went full wolfman, all growly and guttural. 'Ereshkigal has relinquished her hold on me.'

Dillon laughed, the wonky way a madman does in the movies. 'They're coming for you. You're a dead freak walking. And I hope they make it hurt, man.'

Kira felt it before she saw it. The swell of rage catapulting across the space that separated her from Azrael.

'No, Az don't—'

Azrael's shoulders twisted. A sharp crack rang out, and Dillon's body went limp.

'Oh Jesus.' Kira pressed her hands to her mouth.

This shit was getting out of control. Lunch was staying down through sheer willpower alone. Az let Dillon drop to the ground. And the flop of his head to one side was a sight Kira wouldn't be forgetting anytime soon. Blood soaked the tatters of Az's shirt. Way too much blood for one day. Hell, for a lifetime. Time to get the fuck out of here and head somewhere—'Oh god, Vail.' Kira cried. 'They said they found him.'

If they had hurt the kid too, she was going to lose her shit all over the place.

Azrael placed a firm hand on her shoulder, drawing her towards him. 'We will go to him.' The metal wings returned. Whisper quiet. And he slid his arm beneath her knees, lifting her in his arms.

'Whoa, dude. What are you . . .'

It was pretty obvious what the dude was doing. Flying her away. From the chunks and the spilled guts. They drew up high off the ground, the lengths of metal that made up his wings moving with quicksilver speed and heading them towards the low rise where she'd left Vail. This was so not her gig, being cradled like a child. But it was the furthest she'd ever felt from being a kid. She fit into his arms and against his chest like a jigsaw piece against its partner.

Azrael guided them low through the pine forest that separated the road from the paddock beyond. He tilted his body to one side, then the other, negotiating the trunks and branches. And damn if she didn't know exactly which way he was going to go before he went there. Kira didn't bother to hold tight. Didn't need to. Her slice-and-dice buddy would never drop her. If this was how that Gilgamesh king guy had felt, Kira understood now why he'd decided to fuck with the gods. He was goddamn invincible.

The afternoon was dying. The ground was already marked with shadows, and the sun just a sliver above the distant mountain range.

They broke clear of the trees. Ahead was the small hill where she'd abandoned Vail.

'No, no, no.' Kira wriggled in Az's grip. 'Put me down, put me down.'

Vail lay at the base of the hill, not far from where a Hummer sat with doors wide open. A couple of grimalkin smouldered in the green grass, tiny flames flickering from within gaping tears in their sides. Their handlers lay a short distance away, two body-armoured guards face down in the dirt.

And standing in the middle of it all, like a messed-up conductor whose orchestra had just imploded, was the dark-haired woman in an immaculate snow-white coat and leopard print heels.

Tamas -36

After the third minute, Tamas decided there was really no need for the repeated touches of the man's fingertips against his brow. Each press of skin made the sweat build beneath his armpits.

'How about that, sir?' Tight dark curls and the hint of garlic on his breath, the man – Stanton, according to his ID – asked the question for the fifth time.

'That's fine.' Tamas cleared his throat. 'I said that's fine.'

The man's hand dropped from the VR headset he'd been adjusting around Tamas's bandages.

'Would you like any assistance with the operation of the—'

'No.' Tamas kept his eyes locked on the widescreen TV set at the end of his bed. 'I don't require your assistance. Just go.'

His pulse raced with the thrill of it. Seven words spoken in a row without a stutter. Tamas waited until he heard the swoosh of closing doors before releasing a deep sigh and slumping back against his pillow. The doctor had warned him against doing too much so soon after surgery, and Tamas's trip to the Orientation Room had taken it out of him. The energy drain wasn't entirely physical. He wiped at his forehead. Pressing his lips and swallowing the bitterness of the memory of Blake screaming at him, ranting about bringing his world down. But her threats weren't what made the memory bitter. It was his reaction. Racing out of there like a kid running from the principal.

Tamas sat up, waited for the dizziness to settle, and adjusted the VR headset against his forehead. Blake could scream all she wanted. The only person bringing down worlds now was him. He tilted the visor over his eyes, submerging himself into the virtual-reality world awaiting him. The bandaging on his head didn't make for a perfect fit, so his view was lopsided.

'Welcome aboard, sir.' Reuben sat facing him.

Not him exactly, rather the AI positioned in the helicopter's cabin. Tamas nodded, and the AI unit moved in conjunction. The body he controlled had none of the refinement of the Four or Azrael. This was no carapace, no hollow metal shell confining a preternatural force. It was, quite simply, a robot, a humanoid AI that was Tamas's front-row seat on this reconnaissance mission. In the past he had travelled this way with the Syranians when they were sent out on black operations. From the comfort of his Facility room, Tamas could explore the world. Safe. Isolated. And always within reach of creature comforts. The only way to travel.

Tamas disengaged the full-body capabilities of his avatar, so that when he leaned back against his pillow, the robot in the helicopter would not imitate him.

'Estimated arrival?' he asked. Tamas looked out on the virtual world around him with an ease that would escape him were he actually there. For once, he was unperturbed by the brusque, hard stares of the five-person task force.

'Ten minutes to location, sir,' Reuben said.

Tamas took in the mess of abrasions on his bodyguard's cheeks, the odd shade of brown of his lips. Reuben's eyes were covered by reflective sunglasses despite the dimness of the cabin, and he clutched the edge of his seat. In the privacy of his own room, Tamas's fingers sank into the bedclothes, a jab of guilt coming from seeing the discomfort Reuben was in.

'How are you holding up?' Tamas's voice flowed calmly through the private comms link.

The pause was brief but significant. 'Fine. Though there is no doubt of the . . . urgency . . . of this mission. It has been made quite clear to me.' He hunched forward, lowering his head, breathing out a slow, heavy breath.

Understanding how much Reuben would loathe being stared at while in obvious discomfort, Tamas busied himself with observing the others assembled: four other armed, black-suited guards, only their eyes visible behind balaclavas, even their hands covered in gloves. Exactly as Captain Nex and his alien crew had dressed on their boredom-alleviating missions. With their ocular contacts in place, the Syranians became anonymous – though impressively lithe and tall – soldiers in the field.

Reuben's strained voice startled him. 'I know the utukku are tracing Kira's DNA, but something has shifted. They have grown far more . . . emphatic . . . that I pursue this direction. A couple of hours ago, they went ballistic. So much so that I couldn't make any sense of the direction they wanted us to go in. I blacked out once or twice before we finally set a northern path from Beleiro—'

'And there was a secondary stop?'

Reuben nodded. 'That's right. A rest stop, the middle of nowhere. But there was nothing there. Just a billboard and a block of restrooms. The Lucentshield detectors got nothing, not like at the hotel. If Kira stopped there with the gallu, there was no trace. But the…utttuku…reacted just like they are now.' He scratched at the back of his hand, angry welts evident on his dark skin. 'Like it is going to bubble right out of my skin. I had no choice but to stop, and it seemed none too pleased to find nothing there.' An uncertain waver clung to his voice. But it was not the time for reassurances.

'The team that was sent to Beleiro after Kira's name came up in relation to those deaths . . . where are they now?'

A search at the hotel had revealed little except the location of the inhibitor bracelet Kira must have been using on Azrael. Fake federal ID's had seen it removed from police hands with relative ease. It was now hidden beneath the material of Reuben's jacket, snug around his wrist. It was coded to pair with Azrael's carapace alone. Considering Blake's position, she was unlikely to reveal if a copy existed. Certainly not likely to assist in coding a second bracelet.

'The Arc Team are on the ground, following in our path. I've instructed Dillon to keep an eye out for anything roadside that's outstanding. Kira isn't doing this on her own. Someone got her out of the hotel, we know that much. The CCTV footage is a mess, I don't believe that's a coincidence.'

Tamas was grateful his AI's smooth panel face didn't betray the scowl resting on his own. Reuben would see twin pools of black, unblinking. No lips pressed tight, no eyebrows knitted with frustration. How Kira had managed to elude them from the moment she'd stepped out of the Facility with Azrael was beyond him. Even with Blake's help. Kira, who lusted after the spotlight the same way she did bed partners, and who had the trash media mesmerised, had managed to vanish.

All at once, Reuben threw off his harness and staggered up behind the pilot, gripping onto the high-backed seat as though his life depended on it.

'Here. Here. Go down. Go down to that farmhouse.' A sharp intake of breath escaped him, and he fell to his knees. 'Down. Down.'

The helicopter tilted forward, the pilot following orders and taking them down to where a farmhouse sprawled atop a hill. Tamas's thoughts brought his avatar to its feet, and he guided it the short distance to where Reuben leaned against the pilot's seat. With autocorrecting stabilisers, Tamas's avatar was unhindered by the movement of the aircraft.

'Reuben –'

'I'm fine. Just give me a minute. You should go. This is it. This is where we should be.'

The pilot's voice rumbled through the comms, barely audible under a sudden slew of static. 'Sirs, we've lost contact with the Arc team. Comms link with Dillon and Alexeev has disengaged.'

'Not a priority,' Reuben hissed. Blood ran from one nostril. 'Open the doors. Now.'

His move to the opening doorway was far from graceful, but he managed it, leaning against the frame to shout his men ahead of him. 'Go, surround the premises.'

Tamas followed behind the five guards, his thoughts directing the avatar from the helicopter. Dust swirled, thick as fog, and crackling interference stormed through the comms. Two people strode out onto the wide veranda that encased the house. The guards fell into offensive stances, fanning out to either side of Tamas's avatar. Weapons raised, their shouts were barely audible beneath the rumble of the aircraft.

'Hands up!'

'On your knees!'

'Get down!'

The duo either could not hear the commands or chose not to follow them. A man dressed in a hideous green kaftan, with a beard as white as snow, stood beside a woman with hair to match his beard. Her tan was ludicrously orange, even from this distance, and the lime green clothing she wore did little to dampen the effect.

'Take them.' Tamas shouted into static that seemed determined to burst his eardrums. 'The rest of you spread out.'

But no one moved. The interference in the comms was nearly unbearable. Tamas urged the avatar forward. A sharp pain raced from his head wound, and he pressed back against the pile of pillows propping him up.

The man and the woman held something in their hands, what looked like little more than a bunch of twigs. Their lips moved, but Tamas's world was filled with static. Dust swirls moved about him, whirling funnels that grew higher than his robotic head – a considerable six foot four – even as he watched. Three funnels rose in tandem around him. Tamas redirected his VR gaze. More grit-infested funnels drew up like serpents around the other team members. They shielded their eyes, hunching forward. The man closest to Tamas's avatar, a bulky specimen that reminded him of Blake's bodyguard Rossiter, fell to his knees, his weapon planted firmly in the dirt.

'Shut down the helicopter!' Tamas screamed into the comms. The comms screamed back at him. He searched for Reuben. No sign of him either in the helicopter or on the ground, but the debris in the air made seeing clearly almost impossible.

The kaftan fluttered wildly around the man's considerable girth. His eyes were shut. So were the woman's, her arms crossed over her chest, fingertips resting on her shoulders. Tamas directed his avatar's gaze back towards the helicopter. The blades loped around in a lazy rotation. Nothing remotely strong enough to whip up the kind of force being directed at them.

Tamas sat bolt upright in his bed. *Being directed at them.*

The humans around him cowered against the blinding dust, but Tamas was neither human right now nor reliant on human senses. He lowered the avatar's hand, pulling the semiautomatic from the hands of the struggling guard to his right. Tamas straightened, clumsy metal fingers nearly losing hold of the weapon. He spotted Reuben dragging a third person from the interior of the building, a burly, dark-bearded man who was none too pleased about being manhandled. The kaftan-clad man's eyes were wide open now, and he raced down the veranda towards Reuben and his struggling captive.

Tamas sent his avatar forward, weapon sighted on the white-haired woman. Coordinating his grip and his footfalls sent fresh jabs of pain through his skull.

'Don't move!' Tamas's voice boomed from the avatar, but he was screaming into a storm.

There was power here, far stronger than they had anticipated. Or bothered to consider. It was the impossible right in front of his artificial eyes. The attack on Perry should have been taken more seriously. Supermundanes weren't just stirring. They were well and truly awakened.

'Shit,' Tamas cursed at the maelstrom around him. And fired.

The ricochet of the gun jerked his metal arm with a force that nearly overbalanced the avatar. But it had the desired effect. The mini tornadoes surrounding the team pulsed and withered. Debris tumbled from the sky like rain. Someone was screaming.

'You bastards! You bloody bastards!' The white-haired woman crouched beside the kaftan-clad man, his head cradled against her chest. There was no missing the injury, even from where Tamas's avatar stood. He had somehow managed to hit a moving target. In the head.

Tamas gagged where he lay in his bed. He pressed a hand to his mouth, and the avatar followed suit. The head wound was unsurvivable. A mess of jagged bone and ruined flesh.

Fresh screams filled the air. Tamas wrenched his gaze from the kaftan man's shattered skull. Reuben held the bearded man up against the wall of the house, something that must have taken enormous effort considering how much his larger captive struggled. The screams came from both men. Rueben's head was back, mouth wide open, and his hands were planted on the bearded man's temples. And just as they had done from Tamas to Reuben, the utukku shot through skin pores, ripping their way free into a new host. Blood ran down Reuben's arms and stained the bearded man's neck. Oddly, he wore a blue-and-white apron, something a chef would wear.

Tamas raced the avatar to Reuben's side.

'What do they see? Is the gallu here?'

Reuben brought his head forward. His eyes were almost as bloodshot as Blake's. 'Kira. Kira was here. But I . . . I don't . . . there's something—'

Reuben arched his back, and his hands fell away from the man's face. The utukku, in specks sharp as glass and tiny as grains of sand, poured from his eyes, nose, and mouth. They bound together into one great cluster, catching the fading sun and reflecting it as though they were a fluid pack of sardines playing in the air, instead of beneath the sea. Those few that had moved into the bearded man raced clear of his skin. His eyes rolled back in his head and white froth poured from his mouth as he collapsed to the ground.

In his room several thousand kilometres away, Tamas's battered body shook under the movement of the remaining utukku in his own system. 'What do they see?' To be so disconnected was infuriating. 'Reuben?' He hooked his metal fingers into the Kevlar vest the guard wore and wrenched him into a sitting position. Not one inch of his face wasn't covered in blood. But his eyes were open, his breathing fast. Alive.

The miniature sandstorm of utukku rose up over them.

'There was…confusion…,' Reuben rasped. 'Something about this place…they seemed to loose focus. But he was here.'

In his Facility room, his heart thudded in his chest. Tamas threw back the covers, desperate to move.

At the farmhouse the utukku swooped down around his AI, encircling it in a sand-coloured wall. Tamas moved his hand through the streaming specks. The metalwork became flecked with tiny indents, but no pain registered. All at once the particles gathered in on themselves, gyrating, pulsing and then settling into an unmistakable image.

Clear as day. Silent as a grave.

Enkidu and Kira. Kneeling on this very veranda, both in what appeared to be an extraordinary amount of pain. Enkidu threw his head back. Wings unfurling. A dramatic and ridiculous appendage Blake had given each of the carapaces. An addition that he had fawned over when she'd revealed it to him. Back in a time when their conversations were civil. And the distance between them was yet to grow.

Now, Blake's indulgent design stole from Tamas the very thing he hunted. Great spreads of metal lifted Enkidu into the sky, and Tamas could do little more than watch him drift away.

Kira - 37

Vail lay broken-scarecrow-style on the ground. His hair shifted in the light breeze, but it was the only thing about him that moved. A smear of blood ran along the left side of his face, and Kira caught sight of a long, angry mark down his right arm. She squirmed out of Azrael's arms before he'd even touched down. The tightness of the expanded metal at her shoulder pinched like a motherfucker, and her ankle twinged as it hit the ground, but little short of amputation was going to stop her from running to the kid.

'Vail, talk to me, buddy.' Kira dropped to her knees alongside him. One of the kid's silver coins was embedded in his right cheek. Smack bang in the centre, with a nasty-looking green bruise forming a halo around it. There was a second one in his arm too, just above the elbow joint. And blood. Too much of the crimson stuff. 'Vail, hey, come on.'

She'd seen the shows. Knew where to put her fingers to check for a pulse. Kira sucked in her breath. Vail's skin was disgustingly clammy. And cold, as though he'd been dipped in an ice bath. Fuck. Don't be dead.

Az stalked towards Nina, pluming his wings out like a magnificent human-shaped peacock, creating a metal barrier between Vail and the woman, whose smile clung to her face like skimpy lingerie: smooth, delicate, and liable to fall off at the slightest touch.

Jesus Christ. Kira shifted her fingers, searching for the pulse. Jackpot. 'Oh, thank fuck.' She slumped back on her heels, but the relief was momentary.

'Oh no, no, no.' Kira touched her fingers to a damp stain on his belly almost hidden by the deep grey fabric of his T-shirt. She pulled up the shirt, and the air got real thin. Her head spun. 'He's been shot. What the fuck did you do—'

'Shot twice, I believe. A few laser burns as well.' Nina might have been answering Kira, but she only had eyes for Azrael. Her fingers played at the base of her neck, caressing the skin there. 'Silly boy tried to use his hocus-pocus skills against frightened soldiers with weapons. Never a particularly good idea; humans do terrible things when they are fearful. But we can chat about that later. Right now, we need to leave.'

No one moved. Az's wings held rock steady, the slender strips of metal curved slightly forward – aimed at Nina. But she and her ridiculously stunning leopard-print high heels didn't seem to give two craps.

'It is good to see you again, my pretty, pretty boy.'

The pretty boy didn't answer, as solid and unmoving as his wing barrier. Kira hovered over Vail. No idea where to touch him. Every part of his body seemed damaged. And lips shouldn't have a tinge of blue. Nope. Blue equals real bad. 'I don't know what to do. What do I do—'

Nina laughed, a tinkling sound suited to a gossipy high-tea, not hanging out in a stinking paddock with corpses and a half-dead boy. 'I'm not a doctor, sweetheart. You know that –'

'What are you then?' Az's wings dipped low. 'What is your true name?'

'Oh my.' Nina gasped, clasping her hands to her water balloons. 'You've found your tongue since we last met, I see.' She slid her hands onto her hips, pushing back the folds of her white coat. Black leather pants fused with every curve, and a delicate electric-blue lace blouse did nothing to hide the fact that she was sans bra. 'But sadly we don't have time for chatting right now. Let me get you home, and we'll have a real in-depth heart to heart.' She raised a hand to touch Az's face and he recoiled.

'Back away,' came his throaty growl, one that said very clearly he wasn't in the mood. 'Come no closer.'

Nina fanned her face with her hands. 'But how can I resist? Truly, you are magnificent.'

Vail's lips parted and a groan left him. It sounded like a dog stuck way, way down in a drain, but it was god-damn music to Kira's ears. 'Vail, Vail, we're here, dude. It's okay. We're going to get you to a hospital—'

'Don't be ridiculous, you'll do no such thing.' Nina tried to find a way around Az's body barrier, but he was having none of it. 'Oh, for goodness sake, I didn't hurt him. I saved his life. A little bit of advice, don't remove those coins anytime soon. It's all that's holding the poor boy together. Truly, we need to go, right now.'

'Go where?' Kira clutched Vail's hand, probably too tightly, but she needed to make sure he knew she was there.

'They are hunting you, and they're not using guns to do it. Not entirely at least.' Nina edged around Azrael, her hands raised. Whatever might have gone on here before they'd arrived hadn't so much as knocked a hair out of place. Her curls clung to her shoulders like exotic serpents. Nina shrugged, and the low V-neck of her blouse put the jelly wobble of her tits on full display. Biting her bottom lip, Kira forced her gaze back down to the ground.

What the fuck was wrong with her? This was not the time for tit-gazing.

'Kira, truly, you're looking at me as though I just removed the boy's testicles. You know full well I only hurt somebody if that's what they want me to do.' Dark lashes lowered over black-pool eyes. Lips parted just a hint and Kira had to look away again, breathe into the heat filling her cheeks. 'You should really show more gratitude, both of you,' Nina continued, raising a slender-fingered hand and gesturing to her left. 'Considering the things I've done to assist you.'

True, the two grimalkin had seen better days, all definitely non-operational, their legs ripped from bodies and their punctured sides spewing wiring and circuit boards. Kira decided not to look too closely at the two men lying a short distance away. Equally lifeless. Vail stirred, his right hand twitching as though he were touching a hot plate in his dreams. Kira shook her head, tried to dislodge a creeping fogginess. *Think straight, for fuck's sake. Think.* Nina had a point about the hospital. Gunshot wounds got reported to police, didn't they? What about coins in faces? That was going to draw a crowd.

'Az,' Kira said. 'Take Vail back to the farmhouse.' Step one. Get Vail to people who could help him. Step two, work out what the hell had just happened.

Turning his back on Nina, Azrael folded his wings back in close to his spine, and the rasp of blades on whetstones filled the air. He knelt beside Kira. 'But what about you?'

Vail moved his head, just a fraction, from one side to the other, eyeballs frantic beneath the grey-green skin of his eyelids.

'You've got the flying thing down, you'll come back for me,' Kira said. 'Just go, Az.'

'Terribly touching moment, I'm sure, but this is not going—' Nina's head jerked up. Kira followed her gaze. Nothing but pale blue sky, the tinge of dusk dulling the edges. A cow mooed somewhere far away, the only sound that interrupted the moment. 'Get up, right now. Do as I say. Quickly, take my hand. Both of you. Hold on to the child, Kira.'

'Teenager, actually—'

'Take my hand,' Nina snapped. 'Now. They are coming.' Nina wasn't so smooth and collected now. She sank her leather-clad knees down onto the soft earth, the length of her white coat spreading out around her. The scent of jasmine moved with her.

'Who is coming? I'm not taking your—'

'Take my bloody hand, Kira. Now.' The softness in Nina's face vanished. The weight of a scowl pinned down her perfect eyebrows. 'The farmhouse became a target the moment you all lit it up like the sun. How do you think I located you? Whatever you did there, it has drawn a lot of attention. And that attention has turned this way, despite my best efforts.' She stretched both hands towards them, blood-red fingernails wiggling. 'The two of you combined have made quite the impact on things. We need to go.' Her gaze raked up and down Az, lingering at certain points along the way. 'And I'm counting on you, my shining lovely, on giving me the boost I will need to move you all.'

Nina had whip-fast reflexes. Her hand landed on Az's shoulder before he, or Kira, could blink. He stiffened, chest jutting, and for one horrifying second Kira thought the wings might fully unfurl, slicing her in half. But he contained them, a visible shudder running through the sheaths of metal. Nina's fingertips found the metal of Kira's shoulder.

'Oh, fuck.' Kira's body rushed with heat. Her nipples tingled against the fabric of her bra, and her ribcage contracted in, hugging her insides like a corset. She was marshmallow in a bony cage. Like the buzz of contact with Az, only magnified two-fold.

Nina's eyes widened. 'Oh yes, this is much more like it. It has been a long time.' She tilted her head back, groaning like a porn star.

But it was the melting that took Kira by surprise. Far as she knew, people shouldn't melt. Not unless you'd dropped some acid. She'd barely dropped lunch, let alone anything more entertaining. But it was happening. Nina and Az's skin seemed to ripple, shudder and shimmer, then pour away from their bones like melted wax. Sound clogged Kira's throat, a lump there stopping anything from escaping. A buzzing filled her ears, and a voice lifted from the weirdness.

Was it calling her name? Did she have a name?

Kira tilted her melty head to one side. The paddock was a smear of green, but something moved in the smear. And spoke.

Kira.

Definitely her name. Kira tried to open her dripping eyes wider. Focus on the blob within the green. A dark blob. Human shaped. Dome head. Built like a truck.

Rossiter. But Kira's lips were too sloppy to work properly.

Nina's face drew in closer. Not drippy at all. Crystal clear. Nina whispered something to her, but the words bubbled and floated away. Much the same as Kira was doing.

If she still had bones, she didn't know it.

Kira drifted further down. Sinking into the flow. Drowning in cold lava.

So this is how it was. Death by melty high. Granted, it took the cake over driving into a tree or being pulverised by a headless mech-cat. But damn, if it wasn't the most inconvenient fucking thing.

For the first time, in a very long time, Kira wasn't ready to die.

Reviews are awesome!
I'd love to know what you think of Metal Angels.
If you have a moment, head to your favourite site and leave a
review :)
Amazon   *   Goodreads   *   Kobo   *   Bookbub

Want to keep up with all the good stuff yet to come?
Subscribe Now!

danielLekgirl.com

Fantasy   Sci-fi   Paranormal